This Book
Belongs To:

_____

_____

LOADING

The White Desert

- 🔈 📶 Catanna 🛡
- 🔊 📶 Perian 🛡
- 🔊 Gannymead 🛡
- 🔊 ▪ Pinksocks 🛡

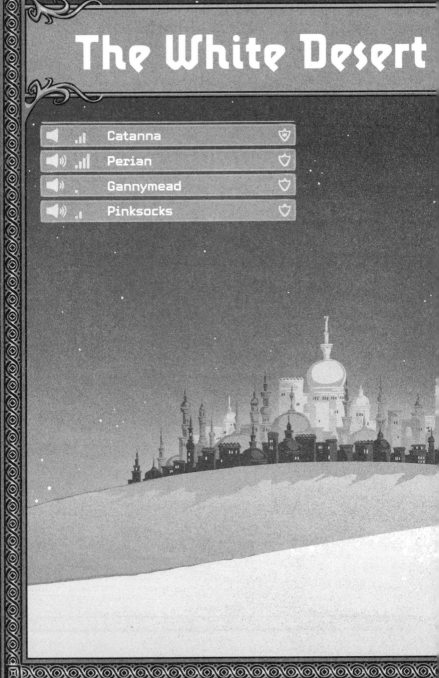

LOADING

LOADING

First published 2018 © Twinkl Ltd of Wards Exchange,
197 Ecclesall Road, Sheffield S11 8HW

ISBN: 978-1-8381906-9-9

Copyright © Twinkl Ltd. 2021

We're passionate about giving our children a sustainable future, which is why this book
is made from Forest Stewardship Council® certified paper. Learn how our Twinkl Green
policy gives the planet a helping hand at www.twinkl.com/twinkl-green.

Printed in the United Kingdom.

10 9 8 7 6 5 4 3 2 1

A catalogue record for this book is available from the British Library.

Twinkl is a registered trademark of Twinkl Ltd.

A TWINKL ORIGINAL

RAIDER'S PERIL

Twinkl Educational Publishing

Contents

LOADING

LOADING FINISHED

Chapter One

Double Life

The quartz spear was nothing special. There were plenty like it at the bazaar, for the right price. The spear's cloudy, white point lay on the workstation next to the pestle and mortar. It glinted dully.

The workstation wasn't special, either. A wooden worktop and a shelf of instruments that had never been used: hammers, pliers, chisels. On the right-hand side was a lever with a gleaming handle. Workstations just like this one were used throughout the White Desert and the Silken City to craft new weapons and armour.

Catanna Brittlestar stood before it. She pounded the pestle into the bowl beneath until the gemstones within were ground to a fine powder. This substance *was* special: topaz.

Catanna had found the topaz gems in a chest on

her last raid. In the gloom of a stronghold basement, she had scooped them into her sack without looking and had run before the enemy guild could capture her. Only when she had reached the safety of the Brittlestar stronghold had she taken the time to examine the unusual blue gems.

Topaz was rare – not as rare as diamond, sunstone or fire opal, but rare enough to make powerful weapons. Rare enough to make Catanna and her Brittlestar guild almost unstoppable... almost. Fire opal weapons would make her truly unstoppable. A guild leader who could equip her followers with fire opal weapons would be revered across the White Desert.

What she wouldn't give to be that leader...

Catanna reached for the lever, gripped the smooth handle and pulled. A sheet of light engulfed the workstation and, with a *boom* –

"Katka?" shouted a voice from downstairs.

Katka pressed the pause button. On the screen, her character, Catanna, froze in the act of reaching for the topaz spear. The spear lay like a shard of luminous, blue ice, reflecting glittering light across Catanna's braids.

"What, Mum?" Katka called back, pulling off the headset that allowed her to talk to other players. She blinked at the bright overhead light. Whenever she played *Raider's Peril*, she got so involved that she forgot that she was a real girl, sitting in a real bedroom.

"You have to help Milana with her spellings."

"I'm busy, Mum."

"Well, so am I."

Katka rolled her eyes. She pulled the headset back over her ears, squished herself more comfortably into the pillows that were piled on the carpet, and unpaused the game.

Catanna grasped the spear and raised it into the air in triumph. A flash of blue light illuminated the sturdy, stone walls of the Brittlestar stronghold.

Gripping the controls, Katka directed Catanna through the stronghold corridors and down the spiral staircase to the weapons store. All of the members of the Brittlestar guild were gathered in the flickering torchlight, waiting for their leader. They were raiding tonight.

Perian stood at the front of the group. Her blue Brittlestar cape swished around her shoulders. She held her bow in one hand and a full quiver was strapped to her back.

"Ready to teach the Gutvine guild a lesson?" said Perian over the headset.

"Oh, I am so ready."

"Katka, come down here and help your sister!"

"I'll help after this raid, Mum."

"How long?"

"Half an hour – promise."

"What was that?" asked Perian. Katka had forgotten to take off her headset.

"Just my mum. Come on, Perian. We're going to gut those Gutvines."

Katka knew the White Desert better than she knew her ten times table. She had been playing *Raider's Peril* for over a year and had founded the Brittlestar guild last Christmas when her old guild had disbanded. Katka and her loyal followers had crisscrossed the desert together many times, sneaking, sprinting and fighting to reach their target.

Today was no different. The raiders ran close to the sand and dodged between scrubby bushes and trees. They ducked behind a dune as a rival guild passed nearby, riding saddled emus.

As the Brittlestars reached the shadow of the Gutvine stronghold, they began to creep. Catanna dashed ahead and crouched within the walls of an ancient temple.

"It's safe," whispered Katka. The raiders' capes fluttered and sand flew around their feet as, one by one, they joined her behind a wall. When everyone was gathered, Catanna cautiously peered through a shattered window at their target.

The Gutvine stronghold was ugly – there was no other word for it. It was a sloppily built castle with lopsided battlements and cockeyed windows. The walls were built of mismatched stone and there was a door halfway up one tower, which made no sense. For some reason, there was also a model of a pink flamingo perched on the roof.

The Gutvines weren't the most powerful guild in the White Desert, nor did they have the best equipment. Katka had targeted them this evening for a special reason: Jaden Sharp.

Jaden Sharp was in Katka's class at school. He

was the sort of boy who annoyed everyone, including his friends. Today, he had been especially irritating.

Mrs Gorman had been teaching them Design Technology, for once. She had brought in bags and bags of recycling from home – plastic bottles and cardboard boxes. She had dug out all the wires, batteries and motors from the science cupboard and had challenged year six to make a working burglar alarm. Katka had just started on a fantastic idea for an alarm in the shape of a dog, which really barked, when Jaden had started being silly.

"Will you stop clipping crocodile clips to Amanda's ears, please, Jaden?"

"I wasn't, Mrs Gorman."

"I saw you. And take that box off your head."

"It's not on my head."

Katka looked. There *was* a box on his head, right over his eyes.

"And remove Rick's pencil case from under your jumper – he's going to need that."

"Who's Rick, Mrs Gorman?"

"*Right.*" Mrs Gorman slammed her whiteboard pen onto the table. "Since Jaden can't be sensible, Jaden is responsible for the whole class missing their DT lesson. Tidy away your things, please. We will have silent reading for the rest of the afternoon."

It was the second time that week.

Jaden's *Raider's Peril* character was a bearded warrior called Xandon Gutvine. Katka spotted him on guard outside the Gutvine stronghold as the Brittlestar party approached. A smirk invaded her face. *Payback time.*

Xandon wore a copper breastplate and carried an iron axe. Pitiful equipment, really, but Katka wasn't going to let that stop her raiding his guild for every last gem she could get. She had been really looking forward to making that barking burglar alarm.

"Perian, let's draw them out," Katka whispered into her microphone. Her hands felt sweaty and her heart was beating fast. This always happened right before a raid, but she knew what she was doing – she'd done it a hundred times.

"On it, Catanna," said Perian. It was strange to think that Perian had been Catanna's second-in-command for so long, and yet neither one knew the other's real name. Katka was always very careful when playing online not to give away her name or any information that could connect her avatar to her real life, in case anyone in *Raider's Peril* turned out to be less than trustworthy. Over time, the pair had found that they could raid together happily without either one sharing this information, and a firm friendship had blossomed.

On the screen, Perian held out her bow and nocked an arrow. She drew the string back and her cape billowed. *Snick* went the bow as the arrow let fly, and *thwack* as it landed in the sand at Xandon's feet.

The stronghold erupted. Raiders poured from every door, including the one that was halfway up a tower. Some even leapt from the roof. They landed like heavy rain on the sand.

"Go, go, go!" Katka yelled into her microphone. The raiding party streamed forwards. Figures ran this way and that, the blue Brittlestar capes marking out Catanna's allies amid the ragtag Gutvine warriors. Catanna raced to the main entrance, pulled back her topaz spear and flung it straight at the doors. *Crash*. They shivered into pieces and the raiding party ran inside.

Katka had a system carefully worked out, and every guild member knew their role: two raiders ran to loot chests; two headed straight for the weapons store; the rest fought off attackers and cleared an escape route.

Catanna raised her spear and circled the room, ready to defend her party against Gutvine warriors – but the Gutvines had disappeared.

"Check all the rooms," she whispered to Perian. "They could be preparing an ambush."

Catanna and Perian crept towards the nearest door.

"One... two... three!" said Perian, and she flung open the door, swinging her bow to face the empty room.

"No one there," said Katka.

They stalked inside. Three more doors came off the chamber in different directions.

"You go left; I'll go right," said Katka.

"Be ready, in case we need to help each other out."

"Always."

Two more doors flung open. Two more empty rooms.

"And no exit from either," said Perian. "Shall we try the last door?"

The final door led to a winding staircase. Catanna and Perian tiptoed upstairs. As they stalked through the shadowy passageways, Katka could hear familiar voices over her headset.

"I've emptied the two silver chests."

"Not much here, but I've grabbed what I could. This ruby sword'll sell for hundreds at the bazaar."

"Gannymead? Pinksocks?" Catanna strode fearlessly down the corridor. Gannymead and Pinksocks were the Brittlestar raiders down for chest looting. "Anyone else up here?"

"Not a soul," said Gannymead's voice. "The Gutvines are all outside. Look."

Across the room, a door swung open into nothingness. This must have been the tower with the door that they had seen from outside. Catanna walked to the opening and looked out.

Across the desert, the Gutvines had gathered. Katka could just make out Xandon's plaited beard and black axe. In the centre of the group stood a man dressed in crimson, clutching an obsidian sword. Obsidian was rarer than topaz and more powerful. Katka wanted everyone in her guild to have weapons like that.

"Right. Get everything you can, then get out," said Katka. "If the Gutvines are outside, the stronghold's abandoned. We're going to torch it. Perian, spread the word." 'Abandoned' had a special meaning in *Raider's Peril*. It meant that no one was left inside a building. Only abandoned structures could be burned down.

Catanna jumped from the open doorway and landed in a crouch on the desert sand below. She exchanged her spear for a torch, which she lit with a match scraped against the stronghold wall. As Catanna held the burning torch aloft, Katka felt her heart slow. Warm tingles spread through her chest. This was it. She'd brought her guild through unharmed, and they had the riches of the Gutvines to prove it.

"Kat?" The bedroom door swung open. Katka's sister, Milana, stood there, wearing her panda onesie and clutching her school book bag. "Can we practise spellings now?"

Katka covered her microphone with one hand. "Two seconds. I'm just about to burn the Gutvines to the ground."

"OK. Two seconds."

Milana padded across the floor and sat on the pillows beside Katka. She sat so close that Katka's elbow brushed against the warm, fluffy onesie fabric whenever she moved, making it hard for Katka to use the controls. It was a good thing that the Gutvines didn't look like they were about to fight back.

"Why aren't they trying to stop us?" asked Perian as she emerged from the stronghold entrance after a final sweep.

"They're just cowards," said Katka. "Now, run."

Catanna put the torch to the stronghold's foundations, turned and fled. When she reached the shelter of the temple, she paused to look back.

"It's been two seconds," said Milana, tugging Katka's arm.

"Don't you want to watch the ugliest stronghold in the White Desert burn?"

Milana turned to the screen but didn't let go of Katka's sleeve. The flames roared around the structure, then the whole ugly mess sank slowly into the ground. The pink flamingo was last to go.

Fire was the only way to destroy things completely in *Raider's Peril*. It turned valuable materials into worthless ash. All that was left of the stronghold was a black heap. Katka grinned. She couldn't help it; it would serve Jaden right for spoiling DT.

"Spellings now?"

"I just need to thank my guild."

"Spellings *now*."

"Two actual seconds this time." Katka adjusted her mic and Catanna turned to face the Brittlestar raiders. "Fantastic. Another successful raid. We got everything the Gutvines had, so –"

"Uh, Catanna?" Perian's voice interrupted. "What are they doing?"

Catanna spun round. The Gutvines ran towards the smoking heap, gathered ash into their loot sacks and dashed in the opposite direction.

Katka watched as Xandon flung himself at the ash, gathering so much that his loot bag bulged. Voices clamoured on her headset.

"They're making for the Silken City."

"What are they up to?"

"We should follow them."

"Spellings! Now!" Milana stomped towards the console and jabbed her fingers at the buttons. The warm, whirring noise that Katka was so used to became a short whine, then the console spluttered out of life.

"Milana!" Katka grabbed at Milana's arm but it was too late. The screen was black.

"I've got ten out of ten two weeks in a row. If I get it again, I get the headteacher's gold star."

Katka stared at the blank screen. "Fine," she sighed. She adjusted the pillows on the floor and took the spellings book that Milana handed her. Milana lay opposite, a pencil already poised over a piece of paper. "First word: *money*."

Chapter Two

Clever Clown

"What was *that* about?" Katka demanded, marching into the classroom the next morning. She threw her book bag under her peg and made a beeline for Jaden's table.

Jaden had a large rubber eraser and a pair of safety scissors on the desk in front of him. He was attempting to hack the eraser into some sort of shape with the blunt blades.

"What was what about?" he said, not looking at Katka. His black hair was too long and it hung over his face, which probably made not looking at people loads easier. He twisted the handles of the scissors so hard that the eraser pinged out and nearly hit Katka in the eye.

"Last night on *Raider's Peril*," Katka persisted, grabbing the mutilated eraser before Jaden could. "You just stood back and let the Gutvine stronghold burn to the ground. What are you, stupid or something? Scared?"

Jaden laughed. "The Gutvines aren't scared of anything." He made a lunge for the eraser in Katka's hand, but she jumped backwards. "It's the Brittlestars who are cowards, raiding a stronghold that's not even defended."

"You *chose* not to defend it. We expected you to fight back. We're not cowards."

"Still, not exactly a great win, is it? Torching an undefended stronghold." Jaden actually looked up at her. The smug glint in his brown eyes made Katka feel like the glory of last night was leaking out through her toes.

"But why didn't you defend it? It was a brutal defeat. You lost everything."

Jaden smiled. "We got exactly what we wanted. All part of Zircon's plan. Now, give me that." He lunged for the eraser again. Katka took another step back and nearly crashed into Dom and Vijay, who were rushing to sit down.

"Who's Zircon? And what's his plan?"

"Why would I tell someone who's stupid enough to score an own goal?"

Heat rushed to Katka's face and her skin tingled. "That's got nothing to do with –" she spluttered. "And anyway, I wouldn't have, if –"

Jaden didn't let her finish. "Gutvine business, isn't it?"

"Fine." Katka took a deep breath. Jaden was never going to let that own goal go. She looked down at the object in her hand. "What is this meant to be, anyway?"

"I'm carving a diamond axe. Give."

"Looks more like a mutant toothbrush."

"Katka, give it back before –"

The classroom door clicked open. Katka tossed the eraser onto Jaden's desk. It bounced across the blue tabletop and Jaden snatched it. "Yes!"

"*Jaden.*" Mrs Gorman stood in the doorway, her face as red as their school sweatshirts.

"Uh-oh." Katka darted across the classroom to her own seat. When she looked back at Jaden, his hair was completely covering his face and his hands were tucked guiltily beneath the desk.

"You will hand over whatever you are hiding immediately," said Mrs Gorman, striding to Jaden's desk with her hand held out.

"I'm not hiding anything," he said, leaning back defensively.

"It's an eraser, Mrs Gorman," said Amanda, who had the misfortune of sitting next to Jaden. Mrs Gorman raised her eyebrows and waited.

"Oh, look. How did that get there?" said Jaden, lifting the half-finished axe model out from under the table. "I don't know how it got all cut up, Mrs Gorman. I just found it, honest."

Mrs Gorman took it from him, silently walked to her desk and threw the eraser in the waste bin.

"Jaden will be staying in at break to write a letter to the headteacher. In the letter, he will discuss why he is not allowed to destroy school property and explain how he intends to pay the school back this time. Now, line up. Our first lesson is in the computer suite."

As the class pushed their seats under their desks and shuffled to the door, Katka noticed Jaden darting towards Mrs Gorman's desk. He reached into the bin and slipped the model into his pocket. *Great*, thought Katka. Jaden was going to ruin their computing lesson, too.

Katka liked the computer suite. It was cooler and less cluttered than the rest of the school. Today, the class was starting a new unit on building websites.

"Does anyone know what 'HTML' stands for?" asked Mrs Gorman, writing the letters on the board. Only one hand went up: Jaden's.

Mrs Gorman looked at Jaden. She pursed her lips. Jaden wiggled his fingers a little and waited. Mrs Gorman turned to the rest of the class. "Why doesn't everyone tell a partner what they think HTML might stand for?" she said.

Everyone spoke at once.

"How To Make... Lemonade," suggested Rick, who was sitting on Katka's left.

"No! How To Make Lasers," said Vijay from her other side. His eyes were wide and shining with anticipation.

"Happy Tortoises..." said Katka. She chewed her lip and thought. "...Meow Loudly."

"That has nothing to do with computers," said Rick.

"Neither does lemonade," she retorted.

"And tortoises don't meow," added Vijay.

"I know that."

"Happy Tortoises Munch Loudly would make sense," Vijay continued. "I used to have a pet tortoise. She did a lot of munching."

When the class fell silent, Jaden was still the only one with his hand up.

"Yes, Jaden?" said Mrs Gorman warily.

"'HTML' stands for HyperText Markup Language," he said.

"That's... right. Well done, Jaden." Katka could tell by the careful rise and fall of her voice that Mrs Gorman was surprised. Mrs Gorman wrote *HyperText Markup Language* on the board. "And what does HTML do?" Jaden's hand was the only one raised, again.

"Go on..." said Mrs Gorman.

"It's how you programme a webpage to show words and pictures and links and stuff."

"You know, Jaden, it's taken seven years but, at last, you've found your calling. Jaden is correct, class, and today we're going to be learning some basic HTML to make our own websites."

It was a good lesson. Katka paired up with Amanda and they created almost an entire page about the girls' football team. Afterwards, she looked for Jaden. To Katka's surprise, the eraser had stayed a misshapen lump against his thigh – he hadn't touched it once. Katka almost felt sorry for reducing his guild's stronghold to ash.

The feeling didn't last. After break, they had maths. As Katka attempted a long multiplication question involving decimals, a sound disturbed the low chatter in the classroom.

Crack.

Jaden sat, stunned. The rubber model lay on the desk before him, now looking even less like a diamond axe and even more like a mutant toothbrush. In his hands, Jaden held the two halves of the safety scissors, which had mysteriously snapped in two.

"You'll be paying for new scissors as well as a new eraser, then," said Mrs Gorman, confiscating both and shutting them in her desk drawer. "I hope you've saved up plenty of pocket money, Jaden. You're going to need it."

Chapter Three

Worthless Ash

Catanna took out her topaz spear. It was a quiet night in the stronghold – just her and Perian. The other members were all busy with their real lives: chess club, history homework, birthday parties. Catanna aimed her spear through a slit window. If she got the angle just right, she could probably hit one of those palm trees outside.

"I've stashed the gems," said Perian. She was sorting through the Gutvine loot. Two bags sat side by side on the flagstones. "This bag is full of weapons to sell – nothing we don't already have – and this one is full of other equipment: armour, boots, cloaks."

Catanna put her spear away and they each picked a bag. "Ready?"

"Ready."

They left the stronghold, bound for the covered market: a small collection of stalls halfway across the White Desert. Business wasn't as brisk there as in the Silken City bazaar, but they could often charge a higher price.

The desert was quiet. Only the regular tramping of their feet in the sand disturbed the chirping song of nearby crickets.

Crash. Katka's bedroom door banged open and the handle slammed into the wall, chipping away another flake of blue paint.

"...and this is my bedroom, and that's my sister." Milana stood in the doorway with another six-year-old girl. They looked almost identical in their school uniforms, except that Milana's friend had dark hair instead of the white-blonde colour that Katka shared with her sister. "She's always playing that game," Milana explained. "She's obsessed or something. Do you like dressing up?"

Katka squashed the spongy earpieces into her ears and ramped up the volume in an attempt to block out their voices. It didn't work.

"You're on the football team, aren't you?" Milana's friend asked. "You went up in assembly."

Katka grunted.

"She's not very good," said Milana, rolling her eyes. She dug out a princess dress from under the bed and threw it onto the top bunk, which was hers. "Everyone knows that she scored that own goal. Remember?"

Katka flung the headset off. "That was one time," she barked. "And it wasn't even in a match, *and* I scored the most goals of any player last term. Real goals, not own goals."

Milana raised her eyebrows and pulled a face exactly like their mum did when she was unimpressed. "Well, no one thinks she's very good any more," said Milana in a loud whisper. She picked up her fairy wings and her panda onesie. "Bella, do you want to be the fairy princess or the bear?"

Katka huffed. What would it take to make that stupid 'own goal' story die? Loads of people scored own goals and the whole school never got to hear about *them*. Why her?

She knew the answer: Jaden. Katka pulled the headset back over her ears and turned the volume right up.

In the desert, Catanna hurried to catch up with her second-in-command. Perian was past the palm trees, striding through a clump of tents. She was nearly at the ancient temple.

"Sorry, Perian. My sister invaded the bedroom."

"I'm glad I don't have a sister."

Katka grunted. "She's all right sometimes, but definitely not when she's telling me how bad I am at football."

"If I did have a sister," Perian mused, "and she told me I was bad at football, she would be a thousand percent right. Sport is my absolute worst thing."

This was another strange thing about Perian. At school, all of Katka's friends were on the football team but online, Perian was her best friend and it didn't matter that Katka was sporty and Perian wasn't. They both cared about the guild. That was all that mattered.

"Hey, Catanna. We're right by the Gutvine stronghold. Want to check out the ruins?"

A vengeful flame flickered alight in Katka's chest. She did want to see the Gutvine stronghold. She wanted to gloat.

"Yeah, I guess we could check it out," she said, trying to sound not-that-interested. Gloating wasn't something that a good leader should do, even if she really wanted to.

"Just to make sure it's really as burnt as we remember," said Perian, a laugh in her voice.

When they reached the temple, it was in shadow. That was strange. The moon cast a white glow over the desert around them like a floodlight but, ahead of them, a huge, lumpy blackness rose from the sand, blocking the light.

"What is that?" said Katka.

"It's not –"

"Let's get closer."

"I'll eat you!" screamed Milana. Bella ran in front of Katka in the princess dress, blocking her view. Milana chased after Bella in the onesie, roaring.

"Get out of the way!" yelled Katka, but the girls pursued each other in circles around her so that it was impossible to see the screen. "Go and be a bear somewhere else."

"Eek! A fearsome, raging ogre," Milana shrieked. She grabbed Bella by the wings and dragged her from the room in a fit of screaming giggles. The door slammed shut behind them.

Katka realised that Perian had just finished speaking.

"Sorry?" she said, wriggling deeper into the pillows on the floor. At last, she had the room to herself. She could concentrate.

"It's a new stronghold. Look."

Katka quickly pressed the arrows on the controller and Catanna ran out from the shadows. From there, Katka could see the vast, wooden walls, the mismatched windows and the Gutvine flags flying from three twisted towers on the roof.

"It's even uglier than the last one," said Katka.

"How did they do it so fast?"

"No idea. Hang on – is that...?" Catanna stepped closer to the door, where a warrior stood on guard. The axe and breastplate were new – made of dark gemstone – but the warrior's face was unmistakable.

"Xandon," said Katka.

"Look who it is," said Jaden's voice. Katka winced. She wasn't prepared to hear Jaden speaking at twice his usual volume while she was sitting safely in her own bedroom.

"What are you doing here?" she asked. Catanna stepped forwards and pulled out her spear.

"Keeping watch on the stronghold. Zircon's got everyone else at work in the city."

"You mean you're the only one here?" asked Perian, her bowstring drawn.

"The only one," said Jaden. There was a pause. An animated breeze ruffled the sand and the girls' Brittlestar capes fluttered. "Why? You thinking of burning us down again?"

"No," said Katka quickly. Xandon's new axe looked nasty. "Where did you get the resources to build it?"

"Gutvine secret, isn't it?" said Jaden. Katka might have been imagining it, but even Xandon's animated face looked smug. He wore a self-satisfied smile behind his enormous beard.

"But we took everything," Katka persisted. "All your gems and stones. We've got your weapons in these loot bags. It doesn't make sense. Where did you get that new axe?"

"Oh, this?" Xandon swished the axe. A *fwip* sound filled Katka's ears and she hurriedly pressed the back button so that Catanna stepped away – but Xandon hadn't been aiming for her. He was just showing off.

"Gift from Zircon. He's promised me a diamond axe, too, but it's not ready yet. Better than a mutant toothbrush, anyway."

"What's it made of?" asked Perian. Her bow was still drawn but she hadn't reacted the same way that Katka had, else Xandon might have had an arrow sticking out of him. "Bloodstone?"

"Onyx," said Jaden. "Not bad, for now. A step up from topaz."

Katka's hands flinched on the controller and Catanna's topaz spear twitched. Just talking to Jaden was making Katka jumpy.

"So, are you burning this place down, or what?" he asked.

"You sound like you want us to," said Perian.

"I can't stop you," Jaden said. "You're not scared, are you?"

"Course not," said Katka. Her fingers were sweaty. She was ready, just in case she needed to throw her spear at Xandon and finish him off.

"So burn it."

They stood in silence. Katka's mind skipped like a skimmed stone over memories of lessons that Jaden had spoiled. It settled on the worst memory of all...

A rainy PE lesson. On the field, Mrs Gorman splits the class in half to play football. The ball speeds towards Katka's feet and she fumbles it. It glances off and rolls the wrong way down the pitch, towards Katka's own goal. It isn't travelling fast. Even if no one intercepts it, the goalie should have no trouble stopping the ball. One tap of his foot will do the job.

No one intercepts. Katka looks at the goalie, her chest tight.

Jaden stands in goal but he's not even watching the pitch. He has his back to the match and he stares, in a dream, at the vines climbing through the playground fence.

The ball rolls over the line. Katka's team erupts in groans. Jaden turns at last, and he stares at Katka. Katka stares at him. This moment will change everything.

"Own goal! Katka scored an own goal," Jaden shouts, loud enough for the whole class to hear. "Katka thinks she's so good at football but she doesn't even know which goal to shoot at."

"It's a trap," said Perian in Katka's earpiece.

Katka took a breath. She was in the dark, blue solitude of her bedroom. She was playing *Raider's Peril.*

"No trap," Jaden said. "Burn it." His voice had a laugh in it, but only Jaden knew what the joke was.

"Come on, Catanna," said Perian. "We have to get to the market."

"Here – I've even got a torch that you can use," said Jaden. Xandon shouldered his axe and pulled an unlit torch from his pack. He threw it on the ground.

"Why are you doing this?" asked Katka. It made no sense. Maybe Perian was right. Maybe it was a trap... but the stronghold was deserted. There was nothing to stop her burning it.

"It's just kind of funny," said Jaden, actually laughing now. It was the sort of thing Jaden would find funny, Katka thought. He loved destroying things: erasers, DT projects, football...

Well, fine. She picked up the torch.

"Catanna, what if it's a trap?"

"It's not a trap." Catanna lit a match and the torch was engulfed in flame.

"Now, remember," Jaden said, as Xandon backed away from the flame. "The stronghold you want is this one. Don't go burning down any others. We don't want another own goal."

That was it.

Catanna flung the torch in a high arc. She stood and watched as the flame flickered against the deep-blue sky and vanished behind one of the deformed towers.

"Catanna, quick!" Perian was already racing away across the desert. In the distance, the coloured lights of the covered market hung like a glittering rainbow. Unhurriedly, Catanna began to follow but, as her avatar jogged over the uneven dunes, Katka heard Jaden's faint laughter beneath the sound of crackling flames. She stopped and looked back.

Fire, like a great orange beast, devoured the stronghold. Silhouetted against the moon, the tiny figure of Xandon stood and watched.

Catanna didn't move. All at once, doubts crawled into Katka's brain like a plague of insects. Jaden was up to something and Katka had played right into his hands. What if the Gutvines destroyed her guild, her friends and everything she had worked so hard to build?

Alone in her bedroom, Katka put her hands to her burning cheeks. She felt a fool.

As the last flames sank into glowing, red embers and then blackness, Xandon approached the mound of ash and scooped handfuls into his loot bag until it could hold no more, just like last time. As soon as his bag was full, he ran in the opposite direction, towards the glowing haze of the Silken City.

Perian and the market could wait. Katka had to know what Jaden was doing before he destroyed everything.

Chapter Four

Silken City

Catanna ran through the darkness of the White Desert night. She rarely ventured to the Silken City, and never alone. Despite its soft-sounding name, it was a cut-throat place.

Katka's thumb ached from pressing the forwards button as hard as she could. It wouldn't make Catanna move any faster – Katka knew that – but her thumbs wouldn't listen to reason right now. She had to find Xandon and discover what the Gutvines were up to before they tricked her into destroying her own guild.

The hazy light of the distant city grew brighter by degrees. Catanna didn't look to the left or right. She just ran – over dunes, through tented encampments, under the shadows of enemy strongholds. She even splashed through an oasis without swerving; her eyes never left that hazy light.

That was how the bandits got her.

Suddenly, flaming arrows rained down from the sky. Her vision flashed red and Catanna staggered as her health bar dropped. She'd been hit. Unfamiliar voices jumbled over her headset.

"Taste it!"

"One more hit."

"Grab the bag."

Too late, Catanna readied her spear – but Katka couldn't see who to aim at and the spear flew, glittering, into the night, landing uselessly in the sand ahead. Catanna tried to follow it, but she was knocked to the ground by another blow. Her health was critically low.

"She's out."

"Taste it!"

"Shut up and search the bag."

"Topaz. Nice."

"Who uses spears, anyway?"

All Katka could see was black. She pressed every button on the controller but Catanna just lay there, her health bar blinking a warning. She was helpless as her loot bag was snatched away and the unseen assailants emptied its contents and flung it onto the sand. She heard every thud as they ran away across the desert.

Eventually, her health bar climbed above the danger zone and stopped blinking. Katka let out a breath that she didn't know she'd been holding. Catanna stood, picked up her loot bag and looked at the contents: just some useless armour, precision gloves and something called an ice cloak. Great.

Catanna shouldered the bag. All that Gutvine loot, gone in seconds because of Katka's own stupidity. Fantastic.

Catanna moved slowly in circles, searching for her topaz spear. The further Catanna limped, the deeper Katka's heart sank until it dropped right into her stomach. Her spear was gone.

Katka flopped back on her cool pillows. She stared at the ceiling, at the crack that wriggled across it like a road in a map. She was the leader of the Brittlestar guild; despair was not an option. She had to find Xandon and get back what she had lost. With a sigh, she sat upright.

Catanna joined a crowd of raiders, merchants and warriors as she inched closer to the Silken City gates. Non-player guards stood on either side, their formidable weapons ready in case of trouble. Catanna stayed to the middle of the crowd, who jostled and slowed as they reached the bottleneck.

As the bustling chatter and hanging silks of the city came into focus, Catanna was snatched to the side by a guard. The animated face leered down at Catanna, grinning. His teeth were black.

"Show us your goods, then."

Catanna's loot bag was snatched for the second time that night.

"That's something lovely, that is," said the guard. He held up a piece of fabric that looked as if it were woven of water. As the guard held it up, he seemed to vanish behind it.

How was that possible? Katka tried to work out what was missing from her bag. The copper armour and precision gloves were still there. The only thing missing was the ice cloak.

Katka looked carefully. The guard's grubby fingers gripped the hem but his arm was totally invisible behind the translucent fabric. At once, Katka realised what the ice cloak could do.

"Now, you either give me this," said the guard, "as fair payment for entering this fine city, or you don't come in."

Katka made her decision in an instant.

"Give it back," she said to the guard. He threw it down and spat.

"Fine. But the city gates aren't open to you. Turn back, or this blade finds a home in your belly."

Catanna turned and limped away. She walked around the curving wall until the city gate was out of sight. Then, she pulled the ice cloak on.

The effect was instant. The watery fabric clung to Catanna's skin so that she appeared almost invisible. Only the faint, shimmering outline of her arms and legs showed that she existed at all. It was perfect.

As Catanna wove her way back towards the city gates, Katka kept her eyes on the guards to either side. She held her breath. The guards gazed this way and that, polishing their weapons with rags. The city was so close, its colour and noise beckoning. Three more steps – two, one – and Catanna was past the guards.

The Silken City was beautiful. Catanna didn't visit it often so it was easy to forget. Sheets of coloured silk formed a maze of streets, stalls and houses in bright, jewel-like colours like amethyst, amber and ruby.

Now, to find the Gutvines...

It was when she began to search that Katka realised how hopeless her plan was. The city was huge, the streets twisted and tangled, and she didn't even know where to start.

Unseen, Catanna passed stalls and workshops, taverns and street musicians. Her new cloak allowed her to float between traders as though she were made of clear, rippling water. The streets grew busier and Katka realised that she was near the bazaar: the bustling market at the heart of the Silken City.

The bazaar heaved with people who were richly robed, heavily armoured and carrying weapons ranging from wooden staves to ruby daggers.

Then, in the throng, Katka spotted a crimson cloak. Could it be Zircon?

Catanna chased the cloak round a corner. The

black beard and obsidian sword confirmed it: the Gutvine leader strode through the market not ten paces ahead.

Catanna raced after him as he weaved calmly through the crowd. A group of raiders swarmed ahead and Zircon disappeared behind them. Under her new cloak, Catanna charged into their midst, ready to elbow her way through.

As Catanna's arm grazed a raider's back, she froze.

Crack.

Katka hit the forwards button but nothing happened. On the screen, Catanna's clear, watery skin was hardening into shimmering, white ice.

"Why can't I move?" Katka muttered to herself. She pressed every button on the controller again and again but Catanna didn't react. Crowds of raiders swarmed around her, heedless. Others stopped to stare; Catanna wasn't invisible any more. Was it that brush with the raider that had turned Catanna to ice?

It seemed like she had been standing there for an age when, at last, a sound like icicles falling in a cave overwhelmed the burble of the crowd. Ice crystals fell away until Catanna was once more liquid and invisible.

Zircon had vanished. Katka stared down the street ahead. She saw green, blue and purple but no hint of red. Where had he gone?

Catanna dodged and darted through the crowd and, this time, Katka was careful to touch no one. Alleys flashed by on either side and she glanced down each without stopping. She nearly missed the glimpse of red and had to backtrack.

There he was: a cloaked, red figure in the deep shadows of a particularly dingy alleyway. Catanna rushed down it as Zircon disappeared through an open door to one side.

When Catanna reached the doorway, she found a ragged silk curtain. She raised a transparent arm to draw it aside and inched into the gloom beyond.

Lights flashed and voices clamoured. Inside,

the room was crowded with Gutvine warriors. Veiled by her cloak, Catanna stepped back into a shadowy corner, where no one was likely to touch her, and drank it all in.

Loot bags littered the floor. The flashes came from workstations around the walls – five, six, seven of them – but they weren't ordinary workstations. Instead of wood, they were made of something dark and glittery, like granite, but that wasn't the strangest thing about them. Katka watched as Gutvine warriors filled the mortar bowls with ashes. They didn't grind the ashes with pestles or even lay weapons on the worktops, like you were supposed to. They simply pulled the levers.

There was a flash and a *bang*! Then, on the worktops, appeared gemstones – piles of them, all rare and unusual.

"Is that enough?" said a warrior standing beside a workstation heaped with glittering, multicoloured gems. Katka had never seen such riches in all her time playing *Raider's Peril*.

Suddenly, text appeared on the screen. Zircon

was typing his reply.

```
[20:04] Zircon117:
NO SUCH THING AS ENOUGH. KEEP GOING UNTIL
THE CHESTS ARE FULL.
```

It was unusual for players to type messages instead of using a microphone – too time-consuming in the middle of an eventful raid – but some players used it because they didn't have microphones. Was Zircon one of those players?

```
[20:04] Zircon117:
WE NEED DIAMOND. LOTS OF IT.
```

What were these magical workstations that created precious gems from ashes? And where could Katka get one for her guild?

```
[20:05] Zircon117:
AND DON'T FORGET WE NEED THE FIRE OPAL
CHEST FULL BY TONIGHT.
```

Katka's heart fluttered. Fire opal?

Zircon strode to an unmanned table.

> *[20:05]* Zircon117:
> WHY IS NO ONE AT THIS WORKSTATION? WE'RE
> NOT WORKING AT FULL CAPACITY.

"Sorry, Zircon," came a voice that Katka recognised. Jaden was here. "Just checking the chests. Did you know that we have plenty of diamond already? Enough to make my axe…"

> *[20:06]* Zircon117:
> FORGET YOUR AXE, XANDON. FIRE OPAL IS OUR
> TOP PRIORITY. GET WORKING.

"As if getting the stronghold burnt down wasn't enough," Jaden muttered. His character, Xandon, shuffled to the empty workstation and filled the bowl with ash.

The Gutvines could craft fire opal? Perhaps this was Catanna's chance to steal some and make her own fire opal spear. After all, she was weaponless. If she had equipment like that, Brittlestar raids would be a piece of cake. Soon, the Brittlestars would be feared in every corner of the White Desert.

Catanna crept forwards. The fire opal chest was

in the opposite corner. If she could just reach it, maybe she could steal the gems and run before anyone caught her. As she inched over the floor, however, a warrior carrying a sack of ash ran across the room. Catanna jumped to the side and flew straight into Zircon.

At the *crack* of Catanna's skin turning to ice, Katka nearly dropped her controller.

[20:08] Zircon117:
A SPY!

Katka pressed her thumbs on the buttons, but there was nothing she could do until her skin melted. An axe flew towards her and – *crash* – her ice skin shattered. Her health fell to half. She wasn't ice, she wasn't water, and the whole horde of Gutvines could see her.

Fortunately, she could at least move. Before the Gutvines could ready their weapons, Catanna fled through the door and dashed into the sprawling maze of the Silken City.

Chapter Five

Unsatisfying Answers

Katka stood beside the football pitch as a neon-yellow football sailed overhead. She tensed, ready to chase after it, then stopped herself. They boys never let her play any more.

It was year six versus year five. Jaden was there but Katka didn't think he was really playing, either. He was just getting in everyone's way. It was Jaden who had kicked the ball off the pitch, and she was sure that he had done it on purpose. The boys still let *him* play, though.

Vijay ran after the ball and lobbed it back towards his teammates. Jaden went in for a tackle, even though he was tackling his own side. Rick laughed, shoved him and kicked the ball towards the goal. It flew past the goalie's ear, bounced between the two jumpers marking out goalposts and hit the fence with a *clang*. Water droplets showered down from the tree above and splattered onto the goalie's head.

"GOAL!" yelled Rick. He ran a lap of the pitch as the other year six boys leapt onto him.

Jaden didn't bother celebrating. He kicked at a puddle and sprayed water halfway up his trouser leg. As far as Katka knew, Jaden didn't really like football. He wasn't any good at it.

Katka leaned on the cool, metal bench. She knew that she shouldn't be here. She was just torturing herself, watching the boys play when they wouldn't let her join in, but she needed to ask Jaden something.

"Jaden!" she called as he loped over to grab his water bottle from the bench.

"I'm busy."

"You're not even playing properly. You're not meant to tackle your own team."

"Well, at least I haven't scored any own goals," he said. He sucked hard on his bottle, then let the air back in with a *squelch*. "Go and play with your own friends."

"I need to ask you about something," said Katka.

"Well, don't bother." Jaden plonked his water bottle on the bench.

"It's about *Raider's Peril*."

"Not interested," he called back as he ran onto the pitch, intercepted the ball and kicked it straight up into the air, where it spun like a neon sun. Katka couldn't tell whether he had done it on purpose or not.

Jaden couldn't avoid Katka forever. In maths, Mrs Gorman sorted them into groups to conduct a survey. Jaden and Katka were in the same group.

"Jaden, what were those workstations?"

"What workstations?" Jaden muttered. He was in charge of the clipboard that they were using for gathering data.

"The weird, dark workstations."

"I don't know what you're talking about," he said. "Angel, what's your favourite pizza topping?"

Angel was clutching her own clipboard. Her group's survey was about ice cream flavours but Angel seemed more interested in doodling pictures of smiling ice cream cones than collecting data.

"Uh," she said, putting the end of her pink highlighter to her head. "Veggie supreme."

"That's not actually an option," said Jaden. "I'll just put you down for 'cabbage and rotten egg'."

"Gross," Angel made a face. "That's not a pizza flavour."

"Well, it's on here, so it must be. Or do you prefer 'garlic snail'?"

"You're disgusting."

"Jaden." Katka pulled the pencil from his hand so that he had to listen. "You *do* know. Those magical workstations that turn ashes into diamonds and fire opals and stuff. Where did the Gutvines get them?"

"So you admit to sneaking into our workshop to spy?" Jaden turned and flopped his hair back to stare at her. "Better hope that the Brittlestar stronghold is well defended. Zircon will be very interested when I tell him that I know who you are. Might even upgrade my axe from onyx to diamond." Jaden reached down to pick up another pencil from one of the desks. It wasn't his desk or his pencil but that didn't stop him.

"I looked in the *Raider's Peril* handbook and I searched the message boards. I tried about a hundred search terms. That workstation is nowhere. It doesn't exist."

"It obviously does exist," said Jaden. "The Gutvines have seven. Nadiyah, what's your favourite pizza topping?"

"Cheese and tomato."

"I'll put you down for our special 'nothing, not even bread' pizza." Jaden made a mark on his sheet and marched towards the book corner.

"Is that why you keep letting us burn your strongholds down?" Katka said, almost tripping over a chair in her attempts to keep up with him. "To get the ashes for your magical workstations?"

"They're not magical," said Jaden. He thumped the clipboard down on top of the bookcase, knocking down Mrs Gorman's display of Crime and Punishment books. "They're just a mod. Zircon took the standard workstation, he modified the code a bit and now it turns ash into rare gems. No big deal. People make mods all the time."

"I know," Katka frowned. "Why are you getting defensive?"

"No reason. Felix, what's your favourite pizza?"

Katka peered over Jaden's arm at the piece of paper on the clipboard. He hadn't written down 'cabbage and rotten egg' or 'garlic snails'. He just had a list of ordinary pizza toppings, with one tally mark beside 'veggie' and another mark beside 'cheese and tomato'.

There wasn't much to do that lesson except for trailing around after Jaden. He did all the asking and wouldn't let Katka touch the clipboard, so she had plenty of time to think.

She thought about what her guild could do with a modified workstation. They could make hundreds of rare gems and equip every Brittlestar with powerful armour and weapons. Each raider could have their own gemstone: Gannymead could have emerald and Pinksocks could have red beryl. Perian, as second in command, would get diamond, but Katka would save fire opal for herself.

Of course, first, they would have to burn something.

"Jaden?"

"What?" His tally chart was nearly complete, now. Once their data was gathered, they had to calculate each option as a percentage and make a pie chart.

"How come the Gutvines don't burn their own strongholds down?"

Jaden counted up each tally and wrote the total at the end of the column. Katka waited. He didn't reply.

"Jaden?" She sat in the chair next to him and picked up a calculator. "You need ash, right? Why not burn stuff yourself? Why wait for us to come along?"

"We tried burning our own stronghold," Jaden said. "Luckily, I wasn't the guy holding the torch. He got banned."

"Banned?"

"Yeah. Apparently, it's against the rules to burn your own stronghold or something." Jaden stabbed the pencil onto the clipboard and the lead snapped. He tossed the pencil away. "Why? It's our stronghold. You'd think we could burn it if we wanted to."

"Why would he be banned?"

"I told you, he shouldn't have been. It was stupid."

"But they don't ban people for no reason." Katka chewed her lip and typed some more numbers into the calculator. Then, Jaden made a grab for it.

"Hey! I know how to calculate percentages. Let me do something," said Katka.

"Fine. Here." Jaden shoved the tally chart across.

Katka's eyes stared through the paper. "Jaden, they don't ban people from *Raider's Peril* for no reason," she said. "I *know* they don't."

Jaden shrugged.

"Maybe something weird is going on," Katka continued. "No one knows that the workstations exist, they're crazy powerful and they're getting people banned. I think Zircon might be up to something."

Chapter Six

Zircon's Promise

"Where were you?!"

Katka was in her bedroom. Her maths homework lay to one side. Percentage word problems were a cruel and unusual form of torture but, at last, they were done. When Katka had logged in to *Raider's Peril*, she had hoped to finally relax but now, Perian was shouting at her.

"You just abandoned me. Where's the Gutvine loot? Did you sell it?"

It was strange to watch the impassive face of Perian-the-character on the screen while Perian-the-player yelled down the headset.

Katka stared at the calm face before her, willing her own heart to slow down and her own voice to stay low, calm and leader-like.

"I was mugged. Perian, let me explain."

"You lost the loot? You abandoned me and then you lost the loot?"

Katka imagined that she was a gentle breeze wafting over the desert. *Stay calm*, she told herself. *Breathe.* "Perian, listen. I know what the Gutvines are up to."

"I thought we were friends."

"We are –"

"Later, Catanna. I'm too upset to talk right now."

The serene figure of Perian dissolved from the weapons store – that meant that the player had logged out. Katka sighed and closed her eyes. Her bedroom was too cold and the pillows felt lumpy beneath her. She stood, dragged the duvet from her bed and wrapped it around herself like a hug as she sat back down on the floor.

She would wait, Katka decided, until Perian logged back on – all night, if she had to. She just needed to explain.

Catanna searched through the weapons in the storeroom. Without her topaz spear, she was defenceless. The best spear in the store was made of tin – barely worth carrying. A quartz sword hung on the wall, but Catanna hadn't levelled up in sword fighting. Perhaps now was her chance to gain some new skills.

Catanna equipped herself with the sword and swished it about in the empty room. She remembered that there were training grounds in the desert. Maybe Catanna should head there for the night and level up.

As she stepped out from the fortress into the dusk, she saw a blood-red figure loitering near the stronghold.

Zircon?

Catanna slipped back into the doorway. If Zircon was here, perhaps the Gutvines were planning a revenge attack... but he was here alone, as far as she could tell.

Katka retreated into the entrance hall. As long as she was inside the stronghold, it wasn't classified as abandoned. That meant that Zircon couldn't burn it down. She wished that Perian were there to help.

Katka watched, unmoving, from the entrance. Zircon strode across the sand in front of the stronghold. He paused, turned and strode back. Katka didn't let her eyes dart away, even for a second.

Eventually, Zircon walked directly towards the front door. Katka held her quartz sword ready. With no experience, she was guaranteed to lose if it came to a fight, but Zircon didn't need to know that. He just had to see that she was armed.

Suddenly, Zircon was standing in the doorway. His cloak flapped elegantly and his face wore an expression of poise. He looked every inch a guild leader.

He was silent. Just like it had in the workshop, text appeared at the bottom of Katka's screen. She wondered again why he didn't use a microphone.

> *[19:53]* Zircon117:
> CATANNA? ARE YOU IN CHARGE?

Now that she was alone with Zircon, not hearing the player's voice through her headset made Katka more uneasy than she had expected. Even though players didn't use their real names in the game, Katka could always hear her friends' voices over her headset, which gave her some clue about the humans behind their avatars. All she knew about Zircon was that his avatar was a man. She had no way of knowing whom she was actually talking to and it wasn't really the way that she liked to play. She quickly weighed up her options.

"I am the leader," Katka replied out loud.

> *[19:53]* Zircon117:
> GOOD. YOU KNOW MY GUILD, YES?
> THE GUTVINES.

Katka started to reply but, almost immediately, another message from Zircon appeared on her screen, then another, and another. He was typing quickly.

> *[19:53]* Zircon117:
> I BELIEVE YOU KNOW ABOUT OUR NEW
> WORKSTATIONS. THIS IS A RARE NEW
> TECHNOLOGY. VERY SECRET. BUT I CAN LET
> YOU IN ON THE SECRET.
>
> *[19:53]* Zircon117:
> GUTVINES NEED AN ALLY. XANDON HAS
> TOLD YOU THAT WE CANNOT BURN OUR OWN
> STRONGHOLDS. WE CANNOT AFFORD MORE
> WARRIORS GETTING BANNED.
>
> *[19:54]* Zircon117:
> THIS IS WHERE YOU COME IN. GUTVINES BUILD
> STRONGHOLDS. BRITTLESTARS BURN THOSE
> STRONGHOLDS. GUTVINES TRANSFORM THE ASH
> INTO RARE GEMS. WE ALL SHARE THE BOUNTY.

[19:54] Zircon117:
BOTH OUR GUILDS PROFIT AND NO ONE
GETS BANNED.

[19:54] Zircon117:
YOUR GUILD WILL REVERE YOU.

Suddenly, Katka felt full of energy. This was the answer. She could restore all of the lost loot to her guild and more. They would have the most powerful weapons in the White Desert. Their guild would be famed among *Raider's Peril* players the world over.

[19:55] Zircon117:
WE HAVE A DEAL?

"Yes," she gasped.

[19:55] Zircon117:
FIRST ASSIGNMENT IS TOMORROW. WE WILL
HAVE A STRONGHOLD READY FOR BURNING. A
FIRE OPAL SWORD WILL BE YOURS SOON.

"A spear," said Katka quickly. "I usually use a spear."

[19:55] Zircon117:
THEN A FIRE OPAL SPEAR WILL BE YOURS.

Zircon spun in the doorway and walked away across the desert. Catanna sheathed the sword. She wouldn't be needing it for much longer.

The next night, the Brittlestars gathered in the stronghold's weapons store. As Katka looked around at the raiders' matching blue capes, she felt her chest inflating with pride. She had brought these players together. She had earned their trust and they repaid her with loyalty. Any player here would leap into combat for the sake of the guild; Katka knew that. Now, she would be able to repay them.

"Brittlestars! Something really exciting has happened. Yesterday, the Gutvine leader, Zircon, visited the stronghold." Mutters and whispers broke out over the headset. "He didn't come to attack or raid," Katka went on, loud enough to drown the mutters out. "He came to form an alliance."

"You didn't accept, did you?" said Pinksocks. "We hate the Gutvines."

"Ah, but wait till you hear what the Gutvines can do for us," said Katka. She scanned her assembled group. Perian stood to one side. She and Katka hadn't spoken since their fight yesterday. It wasn't like Perian to be so quiet.

Katka explained about the Gutvines' magical workstations that turned ash into rare gems, and the task given to the Brittlestars: to burn strongholds as quickly as the Gutvines could rebuild them.

"...and in return, we get powerful weapons. Emerald swords and diamond bows. A fire opal spear."

"Why don't we just ask for our own magical workstation?" asked Croctordoctor.

"Well..." Katka felt like she had fumbled the ball. Of course, she should have asked Zircon for a workstation! "I didn't discuss it with Zircon... but I'll ask later," she added quickly. "I'm sure he'll agree. This is the start of something huge.

It will take the Brittlestars up a level. We won't be just another desert guild any more. We'll build a palace, stable emus, buy a headquarters in the city. The Brittlestars are going to be big."

The raiders burst into chatter again – now, though, their voices buzzed with excitement.

"Have you seen those palaces made of rare gems? Red beryl roofs and quartz windows and emerald walls? We could have a palace like that."

"Forget matching capes – we could all wear matching armour with the Brittlestar crest on it."

"If we get hold of diamond, we can start making magical items. I've heard there are wands that shoot bolts of ice or fire."

Katka stayed silent. She sent Catanna wandering about the room, listening in on conversations as she passed. This was exactly what she had hoped for. Her guild were as excited as she was.

At last, she reached Perian. Perian turned to look at Catanna. Catanna stood still and looked back.

"Sounds like you got a good deal," Perian said.

"It'll make up for the lost loot, I hope," said Katka. She took a deep breath. A good leader owned up to her mistakes. "I'm sorry, Perian. I shouldn't have disappeared. I should have come with you to the market."

"Well, I'm sorry, too," Perian replied. "Sorry I didn't listen yesterday. You did a good job."

"Thanks," Katka whispered.

"So, are we off to burn down whatever ugly creation the Gutvines have sprung up, or what?"

Alone in her room, Katka grinned. "Brittlestars!" she yelled into the mic. "Grab your weapons. The Gutvines are getting burned tonight!"

Chapter Seven

Dubious Dealings

"What's with the sword?" asked Perian as the Brittlestars crossed the White Desert. The route to the ancient temple was a familiar one, now. The Brittlestars barely hesitated as they dashed along shadowy dune valleys.

"My spear was taken when I was ambushed," Katka explained.

"Those crummy dung beetles. So now you've got a sword?"

"Not for long, I hope. I'm only level one with a sword."

"Ouch. And level twelve with a spear?"

"Thirteen," said Katka. Ahead, the towering, stone arches of the temple pierced the horizon. "Nearly there," she said. With a cursory glance over the empty sand, Catanna ran for the temple entranceway. The Brittlestars followed.

"Right," said Katka as they came to a halt in the looming darkness. "We'll approach the stronghold together. We'll be met by a Gutvine guard but the place will be empty. All we have to do is light a torch, and –"

"Uh, Catanna?" Croctordoctor stood beside a shattered stained glass window. "I don't want to alarm you," he said, "but there is no stronghold."

"No stronghold?" Catanna ran to the back of the temple, where a crooked doorway led outside. She stopped just beyond the door. The wind blew sand in graceful arcs through the night air. The stars glittered like jewels. There was no stronghold.

Then, a shout came from inside the temple.

"Ambush!"

Katka's heart jumped into her throat. Catanna dashed inside, quartz sword drawn and ready.

The Brittlestars clamoured. The darkness was punctuated by flashes of shining swords and flaming arrows. Weapons clanged and raiders roared. Amid the yelling, Katka heard a voice.

"It's not an ambush! It's just me!"

"Xandon? Wait, everyone! Hold your weapons!" Catanna lit a torch. The yellow glow made the scene worse somehow. Katka saw ruined armour and bloody wounds. Pinned against the wall, his black axe raised, was Xandon Gutvine.

"STOP!" Katka yelled.

The Brittlestars stopped still, staring at the damage that they had done to each other. Catanna walked to where Xandon stood against the wall.

"Well, Xandon? Where's this stronghold we're meant to be burning down?"

"I came to tell you," Jaden's voice said. Considering that he was outnumbered, Katka expected him to sound nervous, but he didn't. As always, Jaden sounded as if he was laughing at her. "We had to build it somewhere else. Too many burnt strongholds in the same spot would look suspicious."

"Where is it?"

"The Borderlands."

Katka looked at her guild. She wished that she knew what they were thinking. In the game, the characters had no body language or facial expressions to offer a hint of their inner thoughts. Katka had to go off what her guild said. Right now, they were silent.

"The Borderlands," she said, trying to inflate her voice with confidence. "Fine. Lead on."

"There are bandits roaming the main route," said Jaden, "so we go by the shadows. I hope you're feeling stealthy."

The first part of the journey was straightforward enough. At last, the Brittlestars reached the wasteland at the fringes of the White Desert known as the Borderlands. The Borderlands were dirty and littered with the debris of a long-dead civilisation. It was an easy place for gangs to lurk and leap on unsuspecting travellers.

Katka thought about the ice cloak, still stowed in Catanna's loot bag. If Catanna were alone, she could wear it and traverse the whole of the Borderlands, swift and unseen. However, there was no sense in one Brittlestar being invisible when the rest were so conspicuous. Besides, it would be cowardly of her to disappear and leave her followers to their fates.

The party crouched behind a mountain of metal piping. It wasn't much of a hiding place – if anyone came round the corner, the Brittlestars would be spotted instantly – but it would have to do.

"We're nearly there," Jaden assured them. "You can see the stronghold beyond the next hill."

Catanna crept out from the hiding place. In the distance, she could see the misshapen silhouette that she had come to associate with Gutvine strongholds.

"This is Lemonhead territory, so we've got to go

quickly," Jaden added.

"Lemonhead?"

"That's just their guild name. They don't really have lemons for heads. Actually, they think they're pirates. Are we all ready?" Jaden addressed the whole group. "Move."

Catanna sprinted out from behind the junk mountain. Blue capes flapped on either side of her. The path swerved between a collapsed wall on one side and half a burnt-out truck on the other. Beyond that, the ground fell away. The stronghold was close.

The Brittlestars bunched together and jostled as the pathway narrowed. Walls loomed on one side, grey and streaked with rust. The truck on the other side stood at an angle that blocked out almost all light. Catanna was at the head of the pack, her quartz sword bouncing in her hands as she ran. She was nearly at the crest of the hill – nearly at the Gutvine's stronghold.

"Sandlubbers!"

"Get 'em!"

"YARRR!"

Dark figures erupted from the tattered fabric that covered the van. They held knives and cutlasses, each wore a tricorn hat and most of them had a strange goggle strapped to one eye.

"Lemonheads," Jaden muttered.

The Brittlestars whipped out their weapons and pointed them at the strange group. There was a moment's pause while everyone waited for someone else to make the first move.

A Lemonhead in baggy trousers, a ruffled shirt and a red bandana strode to the front of the group. "What have we here?" she growled. Her one goggle extended from her head like a telescope, pointing at Catanna.

"Ah, the Brittlestar guild. And this here's their leader," she continued. "Hear that, me hearties?"

The other Lemonheads jeered.

"Armed only with a quartz sword? In Lemonhead land?" The girl tutted. "And you're not even trained to use it. You're really not prepared for the Borderlands, are you, sandlubber?"

Katka felt her skin prickle with nervous sweat. She wanted to scratch her arms, but she didn't dare take her hand from the controller. How was the girl doing it? She seemed to know everything about Catanna without even asking. Did the goggle on her eye have some hidden power?

"Don't worry. You won't have that sword for long. Lemonheads, attack!"

"YARRR!"

The Lemonheads screamed and ran at the Brittlestars, cutlasses raised. Catanna lifted her sword and swished it down but, however hard she hit, however carefully she aimed, the sword bounced off, dealing barely a scratch. Catanna couldn't do any real damage. All around her, her guild were getting hit, their health falling. It was hopeless.

Unless...

"Stop," Catanna said. "STOP!" The Lemonheads ignored her, and so did the Brittlestars. "We don't have to fight," Katka gasped as Catanna dodged and weaved between angry blades. "We can trade."

"Why would we trade?" yelled the Lemonhead leader, her ruby cutlass slicing into three Brittlestars with one sweep. "We can just destroy you."

Catanna leapt out the way as the ruby blade flew towards her. "Have you heard of an ice cloak?"

"An ice cloak?" The leader froze, almost as if she'd been turned to ice herself. "All right, stop.

STOP, ye scallywags!"

"She's really taking the pirate theme seriously," Perian muttered. She stood close to Catanna, looking bruised but not broken. Several Lemonheads were obviously suffering arrow wounds from Perian's bow.

"You've got an ice cloak, have you?" the Lemonhead girl said, stepping so close to Catanna they almost bumped noses.

"Yea-" Katka started, but Jaden interrupted.

"No!" His character, Xandon, was limping now. He staggered through the crowd to stand beside Catanna.

Katka nearly screamed in frustration. What did Jaden know? Now, he was going to ruin her plan.

"Not yet, at least," said Jaden. "We're on our way to collect some ice cloaks now. We'll give you one, if –" Jaden paused to put his axe away. "If," he continued, "you let us pass through unharmed. There and back."

Katka's insides squirmed. She didn't trust Jaden. Was this another of his tricks?

"So, we let you through," said the Lemonhead leader. "You pick up these ice cloaks. You come back. You give them to us."

"One. We give *one* to you," said Jaden. There was an ominous pause. Katka's fingers twitched, ready to fight again.

"All right," the Lemonhead said at last. "It's a deal. No sneaking off, though, or we'll be after you with our cutlasses."

Katka took a shaky breath. As Xandon led the Brittlestars out of the narrow passage, Catanna waited to ensure that her guild passed through safely.

Katka watched her raiders limping, bleeding and battered. Guilt stabbed at her guts. She knew that they were only computer-animated wounds; she knew that the injuries would heal by themselves, given time. It didn't stop Katka feeling responsible for bringing her guild to this place, and for unknowingly putting them in harm's way.

Over the crest, the Gutvine stronghold squatted like a great, wooden beast. It was even bigger, and even uglier, than the last one. Katka guessed that there was no point in making a stronghold look pretty if it was just going to be burned out of existence.

A group of Gutvines stood to one side with empty loot bags.

"Ready to go?" asked Jaden. He strode over to join the other Gutvines.

"Ready."

"Right. Set it ablaze."

The Brittlestars hesitated.

"OK," said Katka. Catanna lit a torch. She flung it at the stronghold, and it went up in smoke. "Well, then."

"Is that it?" asked Croctordoctor.

"Uh, I suppose so," Katka replied.

"Your payment will be brought to the Brittlestar stronghold," one of the Gutvines said.

"Right." The guild stood and watched the flames for a minute. No one said anything. As the flames died down, Katka spoke. "Xandon, why did you butt in about the ice cloak? I was handling it."

"No, you weren't. If she knew you had an ice cloak on you, she would have just mugged you to get it. I got you safe passage."

Katka sighed. Jaden was right. She hated that Jaden was right.

Chapter Eight

Awesome Pizza

The next evening, a bulging bag of loot appeared on the stone steps of the Brittlestar stronghold. The Brittlestars were in the middle of an argument, and the loot bag didn't help.

"I'm just saying, there's no point in all of us going," said Pinksocks. Pinksocks wore pink all over: pink shoes, clothes of pink velvet and even pink hair. She really liked pink.

"So what do the rest of us do?" demanded Croctordoctor. Katka had never made up her mind whether or not she liked Croctordoctor's pointy moustache. Right now, she hated it.

"We forge weapons, go to the market, catch wild emu," said Pinksocks. "Whatever. You only need one person to burn down an undefended Gutvine stronghold."

"Well then, why bother with a guild at all?" asked Croctordoctor. He nocked an arrow and pointed it at the rough stronghold wall. Katka wanted to ask him to put it away, but in the mood Croctordoctor was in, he'd shoot her.

"Because," said Gannymead, backing up Pinksocks as always, "normal raids involve fighting and looting. We need the guild."

Katka stepped in. "Look at all this stuff." Catanna pulled out the contents of the loot bag. "Amethyst sword, garnet helmet, a pearl bow. The Gutvine job will make us rich. We'll go back to normal raiding afterwards, I promise."

"Who gets that bow, then?" asked Croctordoctor, pointing at the pearl bow with the tip of his arrow.

"Oh!" Perian said. "Can I have it?" Perian loved shiny weapons.

"Sure," said Katka.

"Perian gets it?" said Croctordoctor, his voice rising suddenly to an unlikely squeak. "She has a good bow already! What about me?"

"Do you want Perian's old bow?" Katka offered.

"Not the point!" Croctordoctor released the bowstring. Catanna ducked, and the arrow burst into pieces on the wall behind.

"Croctor, no!" said Perian, notes of panic in her voice. "You can have the pearl bow. I don't mind."

Croctordoctor spoke over her. "Know what? I'm out. This guild used to be good. Now, you won't share equipment fairly and we don't even go on proper raids. This isn't what *Raider's Peril* is about."

He threw his Brittlestar cape on the ground and stalked from the stronghold. The door slammed shut behind him.

"Good riddance," said Pinksocks.

Katka was silent. It stung to lose a guild member – even a bad-tempered one. Pinksocks was right, though. There was no point in everyone going to burn down an empty, undefended guild.

The Brittlestars slipped into a routine. Each evening, Xandon appeared at the stronghold entrance. He led Catanna and Perian across the White Desert to the new Gutvine location, sometimes as far afield as the Red Plains, Slinkertown or the Falldown Forest.

The journeys were often exciting, taking the pair to places that they weren't used to visiting. The main event soon grew dull, however. The explosion of excitement that Katka had felt the first time she had torched a Gutvine stronghold fizzled daily until it was no more exciting than emptying the dishwasher.

The next day, bags of loot would materialise on the Brittlestar doorstep. Each time she saw them, Katka felt a spark of hope but always, it was extinguished.

"Still no fire opal spear," Katka commented on the fourth day, adding yet another amethyst sword to the Brittlestar store. She was getting fed up of waiting. Surely, she had helped Zircon out enough by now.

"Have you asked Zircon for our own magical

workstation yet?" asked Perian.

"I haven't seen Zircon," said Katka. "It's like he's vanished." Catanna added a fifth copper breastplate to the breastplate pile and a third jasper shield to the shield pile. "But there might be a way..."

"Jaden," said Katka, taking a seat beside Jaden in their computing lesson the next day. "Can you get a message to Zircon for me?"

Katka and Amanda were improving their website for the girls' football team. Jaden and Vijay's website was called *The Ten Greatest Items in Raider's Peril.*

"Maybe," said Jaden. He copied an image of an ice cloak onto the webpage. "What's the message?"

"Can you ask him if our guild can have one of those special workstations?"

"Nope." Jaden adjusted the size of the image, then searched for a picture of a diamond axe.

"What?"

"No way. He won't give you one."

"Why not?"

"They're for Gutvines only."

"Why?"

"Why is the sky green, Katka?"

"It's not –"

"Why do you have two heads, Katka?"

"Jaden –"

"Why are you asking silly questions, Katka?"

"Fine. Act stupid if you want to." Katka turned back to her computer. She changed the website background so that it matched their red football kit. "Why doesn't your website have any fire opal weapons? They're just as powerful as diamond."

Vijay let out a huff of laughter. "No, they're not."

"Uh," Katka frowned at Vijay. "What do you mean, they're not? How would you know? You don't even play *Raider's Peril*."

Vijay raised his eyebrows disparagingly. "Play more than you."

Before Katka could tell Vijay exactly how many gaming hours she had clocked up in the last month, Jaden spoke. "Vijay, Katka is a guild leader. She plays more than I do."

Vijay looked as if he didn't believe a word. "Really?"

"Really," said Katka, determined to speak for herself.

"You don't look like a gamer."

"What does that mean?"

"You're a girl."

"So?"

"Girls don't play games like boys do."

Katka let out a huff of breath. "You want to do a survey?" she asked. Vijay quickly shook his head, but Katka already had her hand up. "Mrs Gorman? Vijay and Jaden need to do a survey to help with their website." Jaden giggled and stuffed his hand over his mouth. "They were too embarrassed to ask themselves," Katka explained.

"Very well," said Mrs Gorman. "Quiet, year six. Katka?"

Katka stood up. She cleared her throat and spoke as loudly as she could, to cover up Jaden's uncontrollable snorting laughter. "This is a survey about who plays games," she said. "Video games, tablet games and phone games all count. Put your hand up if you're a gamer."

Katka watched as almost every hand in the room went up. Even Mrs Gorman raised a finger.

"Well, Jaden and Vijay," said Mrs Gorman, "is that all you wanted to know?"

Jaden stuffed his fist in his mouth so that he wouldn't burst into giggles again. Vijay nodded at his shoes. His cheeks were red.

Katka watched Amanda try six different fonts for their website title. None of them looked right. Katka gazed at Jaden's screen. Somehow, Jaden had made his website look really slick. The colour scheme made you think about *Raider's Peril*. The website slid from page to page whenever a link was clicked. It made Katka's website look like something that a year one could have made.

"What are you staring at?" Jaden asked. Katka, unwilling to let Jaden know that she was admiring his website, had to think quickly.

"Can't you at least *ask* Zircon about the magical workstation?" she said. "Even if you think he'll say no..."

"Katka, it's pointless. He hasn't even given me my diamond axe yet. He promised it to me weeks ago."

"He probably just doesn't have enough diamond yet," said Katka. "It's really rare."

Jaden added another picture to his website. "You

saw how much diamond those workstations pump out. Zircon definitely has enough. There you go, Katka." Jaden refreshed his website. "I've added a fire opal spear to the site, just for you."

That afternoon, Katka's mum collected her daughters from school in her work uniform. "The café is hosting a party this evening. Somebody's sixtieth, so I'll be late home," she explained. Mum managed a café known for its gluten-free and vegan cake collection. "Lucy from next door is coming over when she's back from college. Katka, you know how to heat up pizza, so you are responsible. Don't forget to turn the oven off! And I've left my mobile number by the phone."

"I know it off by heart, Mum," Katka said.

"Well, I've left it just in case. And Gran's number, too."

"What kind of pizza?" asked Milana.

"Chicken," said Mum. "I think. And Katka, help Milana with her homework, please.

She has a spelling test tomorrow."

"Yay! Chicken pizza!" Milana sang, and she skipped through the front gate and down the concrete path to the front door. Mum unlocked the door and Katka trailed in behind. Helping Milana with spellings was not on her list of things to do tonight.

"Remember to turn off the oven!" Mum yelled again, slamming the door closed behind her.

Katka threw her school bag down in the hallway and headed for the stairs. If Jaden wouldn't speak to Zircon, she supposed that she ought to find him herself.

Milana stood at the bottom of the stairs, her hands clasped together. "Where are you going?"

"To play *Raider's Peril*," Katka replied, wearily wondering whether to hunt for Zircon in the Silken City before or after torching the Gutvine's latest stronghold.

"But I'm not allowed to cook pizza on my own," said Milana. She opened her eyes wide, in a way that many grown-ups had told her was adorable.

Katka stopped. Her stomach grumbled. She was hungry, too, and the pizza wouldn't cook itself.

"Fine."

"Yay!"

When Milana picked up the pizza box from the kitchen table, tragedy struck. "Katka, I want chicken. This is cheese and tomato."

"But you like cheese and tomato," Katka sighed, turning on the oven. On the front was a sticky note that read:

REMEMBER TO TURN ME OFF!

"Yes, Mum," Katka sighed.

"I just really, really want chicken," Milana wailed. Her face went red and Katka could tell that she was on the verge of a tantrum.

Katka grabbed the box and pulled the pizza out. "We're going to have something better than chicken pizza," she promised. "We're going to have Awesome Pizza. Get out everything tasty from the fridge."

Ten minutes later, the Awesome Pizza was covered in orange pepper and canned sweetcorn and extra grated cheese – orange cheese for Katka and yellow for Milana. Milana put on the finishing touches with torn-up slices of ham.

"I'm making a smiley face," she explained. "You get the eyes, I get the smile."

"We have to cook it for twelve minutes," Katka said, reading the box.

"That's exactly one episode of *Rainbow Charm Twins*!" said Milana.

"You put the TV on," said Katka, "and I'll put the pizza in."

Milana ran into the living room. Katka hovered by the oven, pizza in hand, and watched Milana through the door as she loaded the episode.

"Ready?"

"Ready."

Katka started to count down. "Three, two, one." She pushed the pizza into the oven and slammed the oven door just as Milana pressed play. As the sparkly music of *Rainbow Charm Twins* started to play, Katka flung herself onto the sofa so hard that Milana bounced up, shrieking with laughter.

When Mum arrived home later that night, she found Lucy at the kitchen table with her coursework, and her two girls dozing together on the sofa. Milana held a pencil in one hand and Katka was using Milana's spelling book as a tiny blanket. Mum put the TV on standby and went into the kitchen to check the oven. It was turned off.

Chapter Nine

Clashing Blades

"You weren't on *Raider's Peril* last night," Jaden said as they cleared away the art equipment.

"No," Katka replied. "I had to look after my sister." Mrs Gorman had put Katka in charge of washing up the paint pots because Mrs Gorman knew that she could be trusted. It was a point of pride for Katka that she almost always got the best jobs.

Jaden, however, wasn't supposed to come within ten paces of the sink. "Don't do it again, all right?" he said sharply.

Katka frowned. "Why not?"

Jaden held a pot of green paint under the running tap. "You'll get into trouble," he warned. Water gushed over the sides of the paint pot and green paint splattered the fronts of their shirts.

"Hey!" said Katka.

Jaden dropped the pot. "Oh, no!" he yelled, pulling at his sodden shirt. "Alien goo! Eurgh, I'm mutating!" He tumbled backwards and writhed on the classroom carpet. "I'm turning into an alien."

Katka didn't watch Jaden with the rest of the class. Everything had to be a performance with him. "Jaden can't tell me what to do," she muttered to herself, dabbing at the paint on her shirt with a wet sponge.

"I got ten out of ten in my spellings again," Milana bragged as they walked home from school. "Even Bella only got nine. Mum, can we have Awesome Pizza again, like Katka made last night?"

"I don't know," said Mum, laughing. "What are the ingredients for Awesome Pizza?"

"Well, first, you get an ordinary pizza, and then you get everything from the fridge, and you pile it all on top."

"Even yoghurts? Even olives?"

"Eurgh, no, not olives," Milana insisted. "Only nice things."

Katka was only half listening. In her mind, she was replaying the conversation with Jaden. What did he mean, *trouble*?

When they reached home, Katka threw her bag down in the usual spot in the hallway and sprinted up the stairs. She wanted to play *Raider's Peril* right now. Whenever she closed her eyes, she saw Catanna running across the vast landscape of the White Desert, like the image was imprinted on the back of her eyelids. *Raider's Peril* was the place where Katka felt most at home.

In the bedroom, Katka threw the pillows from the bunk beds into her squashy heap on the floor. She bounced down onto them and started up the game. As the stronghold faded up, Katka saw frantic movement and heard clashing blades. The stronghold was overrun.

Katka knew at once that it was a raid and that Catanna had landed in the middle of it.

Zircon's last payment had included a tiger's eye spear, and Catanna equipped herself with it now. She surveyed the hall. Blades swung and arrows blurred overhead. A dagger flashed beside Catanna and she dodged it, slaloming between Brittlestars and their assailants.

At the side of the room, Catanna turned and stood with her back to the wall. If anyone attacked her now, at least she would see them coming. She readied her spear, identified a target, adjusted her aim and flung it – *smash* – into an enemy raider. The man staggered back as his health dropped. Catanna ran to collect her spear.

She looked around again. All the Brittlestars were here, fighting with every ounce of their stamina. Pinksocks and Gannymead stood back to back, swinging their swords. Catanna flung her spear once more – *crash* – before spotting Perian on the stairs. Perian's arrows shot overhead, knocking enemies back as they closed in.

Katka's heart pumped against her ribs. She felt thrilled and terrified all at once. Battles like this were what *Raider's Peril* was all about – but the Brittlestar stronghold hadn't been raided in months. It was too well defended.

That was scary. It meant that whatever guild they were fighting was powerful enough to destroy their barricades. The raiders had good weapons – topaz, onyx, ruby – and good armour, too.

Catanna threw her spear again and again. Once, as she ran to fetch it, she was struck from behind. Her health tumbled, but not enough to slow her down. She thought about every footfall, every duck and dodge, and made it to the wall again, safe.

"They're heading for the weapons store," Perian yelled over the headset.

"Cut them off," Katka ordered.

Brittlestars surged towards the doorway.

Sword-wielders hacked at the enemy's front

line while archers shot at those behind. The Brittlestars pressed close together, but not close enough; through the swishing of blue capes, Catanna caught a glimpse of unfamiliar, studded armour as two raiders slipped through the crush.

"We've been infiltrated," Katka announced. "I'll follow. Perian, too." Catanna and Perian dashed down the dark passageway. As they reached the storeroom, Catanna raised her spear.

"Grab the weapons and go," said one of the raiders. She seized the amethyst swords, while the other swiped a silver pike and a bloodstone shield. "Don't leave a thing behind. Zircon wanted every piece returned."

"Zircon?" said Katka. Her thumb hovered over the throw button. Both raiders turned to look at her.

"Quick. Move it," one raider said. Katka pressed down and the spear spun into one raider's back. In the same instant, Perian loosed an arrow at the other raider.

"Take that, you fluff-covered jelly beans!" yelled Perian, as the pair collapsed to the floor. "Now, tell us what guild you're in."

"You must be stupid," said an unfamiliar girl's voice over Katka's headset. "You don't make a deal with Zircon and then bail. Why didn't you burn our stronghold last night? We lost a whole day of work."

"We have lives, you know," said Perian. "Parents. Hobbies. We can't be on here all the time."

"That's not how Zircon sees it," said the girl. "If you don't do what he wants... well, you've seen what happens. Now, let us go."

"Not until you give us back our loot," said Katka.

"It's not yours," said the girl. "It's Zircon's. Move it. I'm warning you."

"No," said Katka.

Perian drew her bowstring back but, before she could shoot, the girl drew an item that Katka didn't recognise from her loot bag. It looked like a crystal orb. With a violent swipe, she smashed it against the stronghold floor.

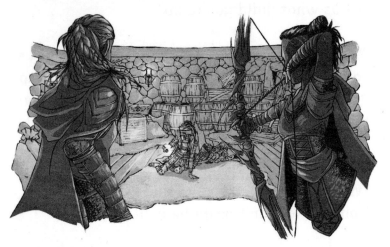

Sound filled Katka's ears – a sound like a cliff giving way and smashing onto the rocks below. The screen flashed white, then black.

Silence.

When Catanna awoke, she awoke to animated stars twinkling overhead. She stood up and looked around. Katka's heart sank like a stone thrown into a lake. Catanna was alone, and the stronghold was in ruins.

Rebuilding the Brittlestar stronghold wasn't a job for one night. The Brittlestars needed to gather resources and buy equipment, which cost money – and to get money, they had to sell loot. Fortunately, two Brittlestar treasure chests had escaped the blast from the crystal orb. *Unfortunately*, they didn't hold much worth selling.

"How dare they?" ranted Pinksocks as she and Catanna trekked to the covered market to sell bronze bars and quartz crystals. "They made a deal with us, then they raided us and stole back everything we earned. It wasn't theirs to take!"

Catanna paced alongside, looking warily to the left and right. Katka was more paranoid than usual; they had lost too much.

"We can earn it back," she promised. "We just have to burn down a few more strongholds. We'll have all that equipment from Zircon in no time."

Pinksocks stopped dead. "You don't mean that you want to carry on with this stupid arrangement, do you?"

"Well, what's the difference?" Katka knew that she sounded impatient but she couldn't help it. She was exhausted. She had spent a sleepless night thinking over every option and she couldn't see any other way. "The Gutvines can raid us whether we're on their side or not. At least this way, they'll give us good equipment first so we stand a chance to defend ourselves."

"There are other ways to get equipment," argued Pinksocks. "We could play the game properly – do what we're good at. We could raid!"

"We will," said Katka. She tapped the thumbstick, impatient to keep walking. "This thing with Zircon isn't going to last much longer. We'll earn back what they took, get the really good weapons we were promised at the beginning, and then break off the deal. It's perfect, because once we're equipped with fire opal, they'll have no chance if they raid us again."

Pinksocks didn't move. "Oh, wake up, Catanna," she said. "When are you going to get a clue?"

Katka winced. She was used to trash talk from other guilds. That was the bad side of gaming.

She wasn't used to that sort of tone from Pinksocks.

"Zircon is never going to give you a fire opal spear," Pinksocks went on. "It's all talk. He thinks that if he ever did give you a fire opal spear, you'd stop helping him – and he's right. You would."

Katka felt shaky. Blood pumped in her head and she was glad that Pinksocks couldn't see her face burning up in humiliation.

"No, I've thought about –" Katka tried to say, but her voice wobbled. She coughed. Her throat closed up. She didn't want to speak again, in case Pinksocks heard how upset she was.

"Whatever," said Pinksocks. "Croctor was right. This guild isn't what it used to be. See you never."

Still holding her bag of Brittlestar loot, Pinksocks walked away across the desert, leaving Catanna standing alone.

Chapter Ten

Unfinished Business

It was Sunday night at the ruined Brittlestar stronghold, but the place was deserted. Deserted, that is, but for two raiders. The raiders wore blue capes adorned with silver stars.

One was building stone walls. They weren't granite walls like the stronghold had once had, but at least they were walls. The other raider built doors. They weren't oak doors – they looked flimsy, as if one little spear throw would shatter them – but they were doors.

"I don't know what to do, Perian," said the raider who was building doors. She stood and stared at what she had just made. It was a terrible door, she thought. Who would want to join a guild with doors like that?

"Catanna, you know I'm your biggest fan," said Perian. "I'm a fan of everything you do. And you haven't done anything wrong."

"Then, where is everyone? Sunday night is raiding night. The Brittlestars never miss it."

"They're just skiving, I expect," said Perian. "Don't want to help with building."

Katka sighed. In her bedroom, she sank so far into the pillows on the floor that she was nearly lying down. "But Pinksocks left. Left forever. And if Pinksocks has left, Gannymead will have, too."

"Never mind about them," said Perian, diligently building.

Katka let her head drop back on the pillows and stared at the ceiling. The crack still crossed it from corner to corner, like a pathway across the desert. If only Katka knew where the pathway was supposed to lead. "Maybe I'm not cut out to be a leader," she said.

"Now, you stop that," said Perian sharply. "There is no better guild than the Brittlestars and you made us what we are. We're organised. We're feared. We had a great stronghold and soon, we'll have an even better one. We always work as a team."

"Hah," said Katka. "Sure."

"We do. The others will be back. You'll see."

Katka's bedroom door creaked open and her mum peered in. Katka sat up.

"It's getting late," Mum said. "Time to stop and go to bed."

Katka covered the headset mic with her hand. "Mum, it's only eight," she hissed as her sister padded into the room and started to change into her pyjamas.

"Well, it's Milana's bedtime. And you need some sleep, too. You have big bags under your eyes like an old woman."

Katka rubbed her eyes. "I'm fine," she said, but she did feel tired – heavy, like she was being pressed down on from above.

Katka flopped back onto the pillows. She felt

like a great wave of greyness could just sweep her away. It was a nice thought. She imagined herself drifting on a softly undulating sea. She knew, somehow, that the grey sea stretched forever in every direction, and the night sky, too. She could rest here. No one needed anything from her on this ocean. She could simply drift.

"Katka?"

"Catanna?"

Katka opened her eyes. She was lying on the bedroom floor. Mum knelt beside her and Perian was talking over the headset.

"Catanna, are you there still?"

"Sorry, Perian. Be right back."

Katka pulled her headset off and shook her head vigorously. She couldn't believe that she'd fallen asleep. There was so much still to do!

"Katka, are you OK?" said Mum. She put a steadying hand on Katka's shoulder. "You've been quiet all weekend."

"I've been completely normal," Katka insisted.

"Well, you haven't played any football with your friends. That isn't like you."

"Mum!" It came out almost like a growl. "I'm just busy with game stuff."

Mum sat back on the carpet and gazed at her daughter, as if deep in thought. "I know you like that *Raider's Peril* game," she said at last, "but you can't let your game life take over your real life."

"Games *are* real life, Mum," said Katka, her face screwed into a deep frown. "They really exist and they have real people playing them." She stared at the screen. Catanna stood uselessly by one of those terrible doors while Perian moved around, building the stronghold alone. "Like Perian," said Katka, pointing. "Behind the avatar, she's a real person, and she's my friend, and I need to help her." She picked up the controller.

"No," said Mum, taking it from her. "If games are real life, then game players need real sleep." She turned the screen off. "Bed. Now."

"Katka? Katka! Earth to Katrina, do you hear me?"

Katka looked up from her exercise book to find the whole class staring at her. She fought to untangle her mind from thoughts of stronghold designs, how to recruit new guild members and what Zircon was up to.

"Um," she said. The class was silent, watchful. They knew that something interesting was about to happen.

"We were wondering," said Mrs Gorman, "if you would care to read your favourite sentence from the story you've been writing today?"

"Um," said Katka again. She looked down at her page. Beneath the title, she had written only four words: *Once upon a tim*. Her face flooded with heat and she quickly added an 'e'.

"We're waiting," said Mrs Gorman.

Katka looked at the clock. How was it breaktime

already? How had she written only four words of her story?

"Um, I don't want to," she mumbled, lowering her head. She worked the tip of her pen into the edge of the table and willed everyone to stop staring.

"You don't want to," Mrs Gorman repeated. The class giggled. "In that case, you can come up to my desk and show me your book. Everyone else, tidy away, please."

All around her, Katka's classmates stood up, chattering. They picked up pencil cases and tucked in chairs and piled up books. Katka didn't move. She didn't take her book to Mrs Gorman's desk. What excuse did she have for writing so little?

Soon, the classroom was empty. Mrs Gorman's shadow fell across Katka's exercise book.

"What's this about then?" said Mrs Gorman, pulling the book towards her. "This isn't the Katka I know."

Katka gulped.

"Do you want to explain? I might be able to help," said Mrs Gorman with surprising gentleness. "What is it?"

This only made Katka feel guiltier. If it had been someone like Jaden sitting here with an empty book, Mrs Gorman would already have handed out a week of detentions. It was only because Katka was such a goody-goody normally that Mrs Gorman was being nice. Katka didn't deserve her kindness.

"I don't know," Katka lied. She had a feeling that the words *'Raider's Peril'* and 'guild' and 'Gutvines' would be meaningless to Mrs Gorman.

"I think you do know," Mrs Gorman insisted. Katka knew that this stalemate could go on for a long time, so she said the first thing that popped into her head.

"It's just, you know that PE lesson where I scored that own goal, only Jaden let it in? Well, Jaden keeps going on about it. He hasn't let anyone forget that I was the one who kicked the ball.

And now the boys won't let me play at break, and the team won't pass to me in matches any more."

Mrs Gorman nodded. "You stay here," she said. "I'll fetch Jaden." She left for the playground.

Katka watched the second hand tick slowly round the clock face. With every tick, she felt her insides twisting tighter. Now, she had got Jaden into trouble, as well. What was wrong with her?

After three minutes and thirty-four seconds, Mrs Gorman returned with Jaden behind her. His dark hair was draped over his face so that his eyes were obscured. He stopped in the doorway.

"Now, what do you say, Jaden?" Mrs Gorman prompted.

"Sorry, Katka."

"Are you going to keep telling tales about her?"

"No, Mrs Gorman."

"Are you going to let her play football today?"

"Yes, Mrs Gorman."

"Thank you, Jaden. Wait for Katka, please. You can go out to break together."

Katka closed her book and added it to the pile on the desk. She shuffled over to the doorway. As she got closer, she could make out Jaden's brown eyes under his fringe. He was staring at her, hard.

"I warned you," he murmured as they stepped onto the tarmac together. Jaden walked close to the fence, so Katka followed him. "Don't mess with Zircon."

"I didn't think he'd send people to raid my stronghold!"

"Nor did I," said Jaden.

"Oh," said Katka.

"Well, obviously," said Jaden. "If I'd known, I'd have told you."

Katka was surprised. "What did you think he'd

do, then?"

Jaden walked in silence for a moment, trailing his finger along the metal fence so that it pinged from bar to bar.

"I dunno." *Ting, ting, ting* went his fingers on the fence. "There was this kid in the Gutvines," he said at last, "on a workstation shift. He put the ashes in, pulled the lever, collected the gemstones. Only, he didn't put them all in the chests. He kept some diamond for himself."

"Uh-oh," said Katka.

"Zircon caught him. Got the diamond back. But that wasn't all. Zircon kicked him out of the guild. Then, the kid got banned from the game."

"Banned?" said Katka. "Why?"

"Apparently, he was selling diamond weapons for Bitcoin."

"What's Bitcoin?" Katka said, pronouncing the unfamiliar word slowly.

"It's a cryptocurrency," said Jaden. He left the word hanging there. He might as well have said, 'it's a hippopotodile', for all the sense it made to Katka.

"A what?" she asked.

"Like online money," Jaden explained, obviously enjoying knowing something that Katka didn't. "It's real money, too, not like *Raider's Peril* gold. It's against the rules to sell game items for real money, you know."

"I know," Katka said. It was on the agreement that you had to sign when you signed up for *Raider's Peril*. Weapons could be sold in-game only, for game gold. Anyone found selling *Raider's Peril* weapons for real money had their account suspended. Katka thought that she knew why: it would spoil the game if people who were rich in the real world could just buy the best items, instead of having to work for them in the game like everyone else.

"But he couldn't have," said Jaden. "He wouldn't be stealing a few measly diamond gems if he had diamond weapons to sell. And he only carried a bronze crossbow. Bronze!"

"You reckon Zircon made it up?"

Jaden shrugged. "That's not the only weird thing Zircon's done."

Katka chewed her lip. "No, it's not," she said suddenly. "What about those workstations?"

Jaden stopped and glared at Katka. "They're a mod!" he said, just like last time.

"Fine. They're a mod," she agreed. "But they're not exactly legit, are they? What if everyone had a workstation like that? It would break the game."

"What do you mean?" Jaden was suddenly sulky. Katka pressed on, desperate to get him talking to her normally again.

"Think about it. If everyone could make a workstation like that, *Raider's Peril* would be pointless. Everyone would be rich and there would be no point in raiding."

Jaden bashed his fist against the fence. He shifted his feet. He sighed. "Fine."

"Fine?"

"You're right. Ever since Zircon invented those things, *Raider's Peril* hasn't been any fun."

"Then, why haven't you left the Gutvines?"

"Are you joking? And get banned like that kid?"

"Oh," said Katka. "Yeah. Of course."

"I'll look at the workstation tonight. See if the code looks dodgy."

"You can do that?"

"Course."

Katka grinned. "And I'll look at the game rules. He must be breaking at least ten."

Jaden rolled his eyes. "Trust you to think of reading the rules," he said. Nevertheless, he grinned back.

Chapter Eleven

Fair Play

Katka had football practice on Mondays after school. For the first time ever, she thought about skipping it. Then, Mrs Gorman stopped her as she was going to collect her bags.

"I've had a word with Miss Underwood," she said, referring to the girls' coach. "She's going to have a talk with the team. She knows that you're an excellent sportswoman, and you shouldn't have any more problems with your teammates."

Katka nodded and, as Mrs Gorman walked away, she sighed. She was desperate to get home and scour the *Raider's Peril* rules for anything that could get Zircon into trouble. Now, it would have to wait.

Still, it was good to be on the football pitch. Katka excelled in all of the exercises that day.

She did the most keepy-uppies out of everyone and, in the short match they played at the end, she scored twice.

"Woman of the match," chanted Amanda as Katka led their team in procession back to the classroom.

Katka ran the whole way home. She sprinted up the path to the front door, flushed and excited about football. It was only as the door opened and her mum let her inside that she remembered her plans to find out the truth about Zircon.

She could do it. Zircon wasn't playing fair and Katka was going to sort it out.

"Juice?" said Mum, handing her a glass without waiting for an answer.

Katka gulped it down in one go. "Mum, can I borrow your tablet?" she asked, giving the empty glass back.

"What do you need it for?"

"Research."

Mum nodded. "Once you're out of those clothes," she said.

In shorts and a T-shirt which smelled comfortingly of washing powder, Katka nestled onto the sofa with the tablet.

The rules were written in confusing and convoluted language. Katka felt her brain tying itself in knots as she tried to understand them but she read each rule carefully, just in case.

About halfway through, she found the rule about not selling items for real money. "That could be useful," she said, and saved a screenshot.

Soon afterwards, she came to a clump of rules about modifying items, like how Zircon had modified the workstations. The tiny, black writing made her head buzz. Katka read everything three times but she still wasn't sure that she understood.

"Mum! What does this mean?" she said. Her mum walked through from the kitchen, wiping her hands on a tea towel. "It's too confusing," Katka explained.

Mum put on her reading glasses. She read over the rules nearly as slowly as Katka had, muttering to herself. "This is for *Raider's Peril*, is it?" she asked, and then "What's a 'modification'?" and "What does it mean by 'resources'?"

Katka answered patiently each time. Her mum didn't know much about gaming but she was very good at understanding complicated things. For instance, when strange warning lights had started blinking on their car dashboard a few weeks back, Mum had simply got out her toolbox, found a tutorial online and followed the instructions until the car was fixed. Katka had complete faith in her.

"I think what it means," said Mum at last, "is that you can change the colour and shape of any item. Its appearance, I mean. But you can't change the powers or statistics of an item."

Katka nodded. "So, you could make a quartz spear look like a giant pineapple if you wanted to, but it'd still have to be a quartz spear, and work like a quartz spear. Same hit rate, same damage."

"Why do you want to know, anyway?" Mum asked as Katka took the tablet back and captured a second screenshot.

"Someone on *Raider's Peril* isn't playing fair," said Katka. Zircon had definitely tampered with the workstation's powers and she was going to prove it.

When Katka logged on, Jaden's character, Xandon, was waiting for her at the Brittlestar stronghold.

"Where were you?" Jaden asked without so much as a hello.

"I had football practice and then I had to read the *Raider's Peril* rules. They're really long," Katka explained. "I found something that might be helpful, though." Katka explained what the rules had said about modifications.

"I managed to access the code for those workstations," said Jaden. "You know when you pull the lever? If you pull it when you've filled up the bowl but haven't put an item on the tabletop, what normally happens?"

"Nothing?" Katka guessed. Honestly, she had never tried.

"Exactly. That's what's meant to happen. But Zircon has changed the code. If it detects ash in the bowl and nothing on the tabletop, it automatically creates rare gems in a certain ratio. Ten percent diamond, ten percent fire opal and some other gems, too."

"Which is against the rules."

"Yeah," said Jaden, "I suppose." Katka noticed a tinge of uncertainty in his voice.

"But...?"

"But, so what? Big deal. They're only imaginary gems, aren't they?"

"And Zircon's a bad person. And this could get him into trouble."

"Yeah, but," Jaden hesitated, "what exactly is going to happen? The workstations will get deleted. Zircon's account might be suspended. But he can just make a new account. And you've seen the sort of trouble he can cause. What if he takes revenge?"

Katka sighed. She stared at the poor excuse for a stronghold that she and Perian had tried to build on the ruins of the old one. She couldn't bear to think that it might be raided again.

"Well, we can't let him get away with it," Katka said as the image of Perian fizzed into view beside her.

"Catanna, guess what I've found!" said Perian. "Oh, Xandon." She paused. "I hope you don't think we're going to burn down another Gutvine stronghold for you."

"He's helping me," said Katka. "We think we might be able to stop Zircon. Did you know that he's made up lies to get people banned before?"

"Doesn't surprise me," said Perian. "Wait until you see this website."

Minutes later, Katka had explained to Mum what Perian had said and had settled down next to her on the sofa with her tablet again. Katka typed *Raider Tradez* into the search bar as Perian had instructed her. The results loaded and she clicked the first link.

Instantly, the screen filled with pop-up ads trying to sell her stairlifts, life insurance and online poker. She showed it to Mum, who quickly closed them all until they could see the website underneath.

It was an online catalogue full of *Raider's Peril* equipment, with columns and rows made up of pictures of rare weapons ranging from fire opal to obsidian. They were priced not in *Raider's Peril* gold but in Bitcoin.

They didn't look very expensive to Katka. The highest-priced item was a diamond grenade at 1.2 Bitcoin. Katka recognised that diamond grenade. It was the same thing that the girl raider had used to destroy the Brittlestar stronghold. Until that moment, Katka had never seen one before.

"One point two Bitcoin," said Katka, when she had returned to her bedroom and pulled on her headset again. "Bit cheap." She wanted to show off that she knew exactly what a Bitcoin was.

"Not really," said Jaden, instantly deflating Katka's puff of self-satisfaction. "One Bitcoin can be worth hundreds or even thousands of pounds."

"Thousands?!" spluttered Katka, louder than she meant to.

"Plus, Bitcoin can be anonymous," said Perian. "That's why *criminals* use it." Perian let that comment hang in the air.

"And you think that *Raider Tradez* is Zircon's website?" Katka asked Perian over the headset.

"I don't know for sure," said Perian, "but if it is, think what that means."

"Zircon's using a modified workstation to make powerful weapons, then selling them for real money?" said Katka. "That's totally against the rules."

"So, how are we going to prove it and take him down?" asked Jaden.

"We need a plan," said Katka. "We need to convince the Brittlestars and the Gutvines to join forces against Zircon."

Chapter Twelve

Unguarded Treasure

Mrs Gorman was on break duty the next day when she saw something that nearly made her drop her cup of tea: Katka and Jaden in cahoots! The odd pair stood together under the trees in the far corner of the playground. Katka muttered energetically, making wild gestures with her hands. Mrs Gorman caught a few words as Jaden replied, "Me too! And if we..." She strained her ears but the rest was too quiet to hear.

Well, well, thought Mrs Gorman. Katka, the first girl you asked when you needed someone sensible to do a job, was hanging around with Jaden, the boy who once ate a slug for a dare. Was the world upside down and back to front?

The teacher took a calming sip of tea and went to break up an argument that was threatening to topple the climbing frame. At least *that* was as per usual.

Despite appearances, Katka and Jaden weren't exactly in agreement about the best way to deal with Zircon.

"It'll be the ultimate raid," Katka insisted. Jaden was stripping leaves off a twig he had pulled from the tree above them. The scent of tree sap filled Katka's nostrils. "Brittlestars and Gutvines turn on Zircon. We corner him in the workshop, take everything we can get our hands on –"

"But Katka, listen," Jaden interrupted, waving the leafless twig in her face. "That website – *Raider Tradez* – it's definitely him. I did a domain lookup."

"What's a 'domain lookup'?"

"You can find the name and contact details of anyone who has registered a website," Jaden explained, throwing the stick on the ground.

"You mean, you found out Zircon's real name and real address?" said Katka. She was almost jumping with excitement.

"Hah. Only if his real name is Fishguts McTrevor," Jaden said. "But I reckon he hasn't used his real name. I did a search for Fishguts McTrevor anyway, just to see what would happen. A load of old social media and gaming profiles came up. Looks like he's been using that fake name for ages. And guess what username kept popping up next to it."

"What?" said Katka, though she thought she could guess.

"Zircon." Jaden's voice was deadly serious, now.

"So we have proof! That's exactly what we need. I'll go to the Brittlestars; you go to the Gutvines. We'll strike Zircon's workshop on Wednesday night. That's just enough time to gather resources."

"That won't work," said Jaden. "Katka, we're not fighting a game boss or a monster or something. Defeating Zircon in *Raider's Peril* doesn't stop him in real life."

"But it'll scare him," said Katka. "It'll show him he can't push us around. We know his secret."

"It won't. You don't know Zircon."

"I want to show Zircon up for the crook he is, Jaden!"

"Me too!" Jaden yelled, his voice almost as loud as the year fours squawking on the climbing frame. "And if we think about this carefully, there'll be a better way."

Katka didn't want to find a better way. She could see the future as clearly as a video playing in front of her eyes. She would seek out the old members of her guild and they would jump at the chance to raid Zircon, the very person who had brought them to ruin, uniting again under the Brittlestar banner. Once they had beaten Zircon, looted his workshop and equipped themselves with the best weapons that game gold could buy, they'd be sure to forgive her and join the Brittlestars again. It was the perfect plan.

"You're just scared," Katka said to Jaden. She said it on purpose, not because she believed it but because she knew that the only way to get Jaden to agree to her plan was to taunt him until he cracked. "You're a coward."

Jaden kicked the tree trunk. Bark dust showered onto his shoe. "Think what you like," he said. "It won't work." Then, he stalked away across the playground.

Unfortunately, Katka's plan did not go as smoothly as she'd hoped. The ex-Brittlestars were hard to track down but, once Catanna found one, she found them all.

"We're the Crocogators, now," Gannymead explained as Catanna surveyed their stronghold. It was green and had crenellations like big, square teeth. "Croctordoctor founded it and we all joined."

"Oh. Right," said Katka. She felt like she'd been punched in the guts. Her old teammates uniting together to form a guild without her? That hurt. "I just – well – I have this plan."

Katka explained everything that she knew about Zircon, and her idea to make him pay for what he'd done. Gannymead didn't react with much enthusiasm but she didn't say no, either. "I'll put it to the guild," she said.

"Shall I wait?"

"We know where to find you." With that, Gannymead slammed the stronghold door in Catanna's face. It was made of steel.

At least Perian was on Katka's side. Perian had offered to round up Gutvines, since Jaden wouldn't. Katka wanted Zircon to have as few defences as possible and that meant stripping him of followers.

"Xandon would have had an easier time convincing them," Perian explained when she returned from her trip. "They trust him. But at least they recognise me."

"How many are willing to work with us?"

"Not many. They didn't say it but I think they're scared."

Katka felt a pang of worry, remembering that she had accused Jaden of the same thing. Perhaps there really was something to be afraid of.

Later that evening, a Crocogator messenger

arrived at the stronghold. "The Crocogators have taken a vote," said the messenger, a rookie whom Katka didn't recognise. "We have voted not to assist the Brittlestar guild at this time," she said. "Is this your stronghold? Not very strong, is it?"

"Out," snapped Katka, slamming the wooden stronghold door. Her grand scheme was falling apart.

"We don't have to do it tonight," said Perian, the instant Katka logged in on Wednesday. Katka had tried again – unsuccessfully – to convince Jaden to join them.

Nevertheless, she was ready. She had gathered snacks from the kitchen cupboards – raisins for energy and crisps because they were delicious – and had filled her school water bottle. She had even dragged her heavy chest of drawers in front of the bedroom door so that there was no way for Milana to disturb her at a crucial moment.

"No. It has to be tonight," she said. "We won't

have time to get the message out if we change it and once Zircon knows there's a plot against him, we lose our advantage."

Catanna took out the tiger's eye spear that she now used and inspected it. It wasn't a bad spear, but would it be good enough? It was no use pining for a fire opal spear now, Katka told herself. That had just been a glittering lie Zircon had used to buy her.

"How long until the raid?" Perian asked. She sounded nervous.

"Still another hour until we meet outside the city. Why didn't we organise it for earlier?" Katka felt jumpy and full of energy. She just wanted to get this fight over with.

"You know why," said Perian. "Not everyone can get online until five. Anyway, I think I know where we can get some more resources. I'll be back in time, I promise."

Perian disappeared into the desert night, leaving Katka feeling uneasy and impatient. To take her mind off the battle, she decided to add a stone tower to the east wing of the stronghold.

She was just designing crenellations – inspired by the Crocogators – when she saw running figures in the sand below. Was Perian back from her mysterious mission?

"Catanna?" It was a voice Katka recognised but it wasn't Perian.

"Pinksocks?" Catanna ran downstairs.

"We came," said Pinksocks. As the group stepped closer, Katka counted seven armoured figures, all ex-Brittlestar raiders. "Croctordoctor didn't want us to help you but, well..."

"...we want to see Zircon eat dirt," Gannymead finished.

Katka's chest felt full and her eyes prickled. *Crying is not leader-like behaviour*, she told herself, *especially at a time like this. Just do what you always do.*

"Right, team," said Katka. "This isn't an ordinary raid. Our main objective is to destroy Zircon's workstations. To do that, we need to take out the Gutvines – Zircon most of all – and burn the workshop down. The Gutvines have more powerful weapons than us, so it won't be easy. Are we ready to cook Gutvine flesh for dinner?"

"Yeah!" everyone cheered, and Katka felt herself smile for the first time in days.

"To the Silken City!" Pinksocks cried.

"No, wait." Catanna ran to catch up with the group already striding across the desert. "Perian isn't back."

"She'll know where to find us," said Pinksocks, with a casualness that Katka didn't share. "We're not here as a favour, Catanna. We're here to crush Zircon. We're not going to wait around."

The night was still and quiet. Soon, they reached the gates of the Silken City.

"We should wait for Perian," said Katka.

"How do we know when she'll arrive?" asked Pinksocks.

"She said she'd be here by five."

"Too long." Pinksocks turned towards the iron gates. "Let's head in."

"She's bringing reinforcements!"

"Or else we go without you."

Katka fiddled with her controller uncertainly. Either Catanna went now, with only seven allies, or she let the Crocogators raid Zircon's workshop without her. They could be knocked out of action before Perian even arrived.

"Fine," Katka said. "I'll come now. But we need a plan of action."

After a short discussion, the group headed into the multicoloured hangings and babbling throng of the city. Catanna trailed Pinksocks' bobbing, pink hair closely as they wove their way to the bazaar.

The group huddled in the dimly lit corridor outside the Gutvine workshop.

"Remember," said Pinksocks, "our best chance is to act quick and take them by surprise. Now, get in there!"

Katka winced as the group roared in excitement. They needed to be stealthy, not loud! Catanna led them down the narrow passage towards the workshop entrance.

Hesitating until the final second, Catanna was the last to cross the threshold. She held her spear ready, expecting to enter a chaotic mass of arrows and blades, but what she saw surprised her.

The gloomy workshop was completely deserted. Seven quiet workstations and seven closed chests stood against the walls, unguarded.

"Raid the chests," said Pinksocks, adapting hastily to the situation. "Get all the loot you can."

The Crocogators dashed to all corners and began to rummage. Only Catanna didn't move.

"Diamonds," squealed one raider gleefully.

"Obsidian!"

"Opal!"

An eerie feeling crept over Katka like fog. This was all wrong.

"See, Catanna?" said Pinksocks. "A bloodless raid. We'll torch the place and go."

Catanna kept her spear poised as the raiders filled their loot bags. Where was Zircon? Where were the Gutvines?

"Hurry," she urged, but the Crocogators lingered.

"Hey, are these the magical workstations?" asked

Pinksocks, gesturing to the tool-adorned tables.

"Uh-huh," said Katka. Catanna took a step backwards, towards the door.

"Is it possible to put a workstation in a loot bag?"

"Pinksocks, we should go."

"Chill out, Catanna," said Pinksocks. "No one's here."

Warily, Catanna took another step backwards towards the door.

BASH!

The blow from behind hit Catanna so hard that she sprawled on the floor. Her health bar dropped to half. She stumbled onto her feet and turned round.

"Gutvines!" she yelled.

The Crocogators erupted into panic.

"The Gutvines are here."

"We've been ambushed!"

"Run!"

Enemy warriors crowded inside, brandishing swords and axes. Each weapon was made of powerful gemstones. Before the Crocogators had time to arm themselves, they were under attack. The Gutvines surged forward in a cacophony of shouts and clangs. Catanna dodged, ducked and flung herself against the wall. She threw her spear, hard. It smacked the side of a gold-armoured warrior and bounced off, barely denting the raider's health.

Running to collect her spear, Catanna stumbled over the figures of two Crocogators already knocked unconscious. In front of Catanna, a diamond arrow struck Gannymead and she fell. Before she could get to her feet, a warrior with an emerald axe slammed it down. Gannymead was knocked out.

Catanna flung her spear again, but it flew wide. They were doomed! Three – no, four – of her allies were down, the Gutvines had more powerful weapons and now, she couldn't even aim straight. As Catanna grabbed for her spear, a ruby sword whacked her in the head. Her health fell again.

"Run! *Run!*" she urged her allies.

She staggered towards the door but the Gutvines crowded in too close, a dense, unbeatable wall. Catanna threw her spear into the throng, knowing that it was hopeless. Another blow struck her and she didn't even see which side it came from. The screen flashed red, a warning that she was nearly out of health. She stepped closer to her spear, sure that she would never reach it.

Then, suddenly, the warrior before her dropped with a *thud.* The warriors on either side followed, each pierced by a glinting arrow.

"Take that, Gutvines. You're all a bunch of banana-brains!" yelled a voice that Katka recognised. Perian! She was back.

"You made it," said Katka. Catanna reached for her spear. Her screen stopped blinking red, though her health was still critically low.

"And I brought reinforcements," said Perian, nocking another arrow.

"Yarr! Let's send these sandlubbers to Davy Jones' locker." A tricorn-wearing pirate leapt into the fray, swinging her cutlass wildly.

"The Lemonheads?"

"I told them about a mysterious diamond grenade that could destroy half a stronghold with one blast, rumoured to be in possession of the Gutvines," said Perian. "They couldn't resist."

As Catanna's health crept back up, she fought with renewed vigour. Now that Perian and the Lemonheads were on their side, perhaps they stood a chance. Swords swished, arrows whooshed and Gutvines fell.

"We're winning," said Katka to herself. "Take that, Zircon."

Suddenly, Zircon was there: tall, crimson and commanding.

Katka wasn't expecting it. She had assumed

that he was hiding, letting his minions do the dirty work for him, but there he was. As he strode into the centre of the room, clothed in sleek, fire opal armour, the fighters fell still. Everyone turned to look at him.

In his hand, he held a diamond grenade.

As words began to appear on the screen, it was like the whole room held its breath.

[17:02] Zircon117:
SOME OF YOU KNOW WHAT THIS IS.

Katka stared. Her hands grew sweaty. She wondered whether Catanna could flee the workshop before Zircon used it.

[17:02] Zircon117:
THE BRITTLESTARS WILL TELL YOU WHAT SORT OF DAMAGE THIS OBJECT CAN DO.

Around the room, weapons shifted, pointing at

Zircon. If there was some way to coordinate them so that everyone struck at once, maybe – *maybe* – they could take him out... but how could they get the timing right without alerting Zircon?

[17:03] Zircon117:
IF THE PEOPLE INVADING THIS PLACE DON'T LEAVE RIGHT NOW, I WILL DESTROY EVERY STRONGHOLD OF EVERY GUILD THEY EVER JOIN, FOR ETERNITY.

[17:03] Zircon117:
NOT EXACTLY HARD, WITH A DIAMOND GRENADE.

Catanna lifted her spear. Perhaps if she just yelled 'Now!', everyone would attack him at once. Perhaps they wouldn't.

[17:03] Zircon117:
IN FACT, I MIGHT DESTROY THEM WHETHER YOU LEAVE OR NOT.

Katka took a deep breath, ready to give the order.

[17:03] Zircon117:
JUST AS A LITTLE REMINDER...

[17:03] Zircon117:
JUST AS A LITTLE REMINDER...

[17:03] Zircon117:
NEVER
MESS
WITH

Then, without a flash or a bang or even a squeak,
Zircon vanished.

Chapter Thirteen

Real Friends

For a moment, the raiders and warriors assembled in the workshop gaped at the place where Zircon had disappeared.

"Where's he gone?" said a voice over Katka's headset.

"Did he take the diamond grenade with him?" said another.

"Protect the workshop!" said a third.

That did it. Vicious scuffles broke out all around the room. Gutvines and Crocogators and Brittlestars and Lemonheads all vied for control of the modified workstations.

Perian loosed three arrows in quick succession. Gannymead, wounded, was on her feet again, waving her sword about at random. The

Lemonheads were attacking anyone who came near them, enemy or ally.

"Katka!" called a muffled voice from somewhere outside of *Raider's Peril*, but Katka was too engrossed to hear it.

Catanna spun round to fling her spear at a Gutvine approaching from behind her. When she turned back, the picture on the screen had changed somehow.

"One of the workstations is gone," said Perian. "Vanished, like Zircon."

"Katka?" Muffled bangs from outside the bedroom merged with the clashing and clanging in the workshop. Katka's bedroom door shook and the chest of drawers that she had dragged in front of it wobbled.

Catanna raised her spear again. In front of her eyes, another workstation vanished – then another, and another, until the workshop was empty but for a few looted chests and a lot of confused players.

"KATKA!"

BANG. The chest of drawers fell over. It smashed onto the carpet, inches from where Katka was sitting, and flattened the uneaten bag of crisps. Katka jumped up, her heart pounding. She'd nearly been crushed.

"Oh, Katka. Thank goodness!" Her mum pushed through the door, leapt over the fallen chest and wrapped her daughter in a strangling hug. "You're OK," she said shakily.

"Of course I'm OK," gasped Katka.

Milana stumbled around the fallen chest. She threw her arms around Katka's waist.

"You're alive!"

"Why wouldn't I be alive?"

Her mum squeezed her even harder. The wire of Katka's headphones was tangled around her shoulders.

"Well, you disappeared into your room," said

Mum. "I tried knocking and calling and you didn't answer. And then I tried to open the door, but it wouldn't budge and, oh, my Katka! I was so worried." Mum rocked Katka this way and that, and Milana's sticky fingers pinched her middle. It was very uncomfortable. "Why on earth did you block the door up?"

"I had to do something really important on *Raider's Peril*. I didn't want any interruptions. Mum, you know that person who wasn't playing fair? Zircon? It turns out, he was breaking lots of rules."

Mum was barely listening. "Katka, that's dangerous. Don't you ever do something like that to me again!"

"So we decided to raid him," Katka said, her head still in the workshop. "But then, guess what! He disappeared!"

"You come downstairs, where I can see you, and then you can tell me exactly what you were up to," said Mum.

"Since Katka's alive, can we have Awesome

Pizza?" asked Milana as she followed her mum and big sister from the bedroom.

"Now, tell me what a Zircon is," said Mum, halfway down the stairs.

If anyone had stayed to watch the screen, they would have seen what Perian did next. Alone in the Gutvines' empty workshop, Perian lit a torch, threw it into the middle of the room and walked away.

"What I still don't understand is, where did Zircon go?" said Katka to Amanda as they arrived at school the next day. Amanda, who didn't play *Raider's Peril*, just shrugged.

"Banned," said Jaden, throwing himself into his chair.

"Banned?"

"For life," he added. He took an object from his pocket and swished it around.

"How d'you know?" asked Katka. The object was white and glittery, and shaped rather like...

"I'll show you later. In computing."

"Wait, is that a diamond axe?" said Katka, snatching it from Jaden's hand.

"Yeah, I finished carving and painting that eraser," he said. "Doesn't look like a mutant toothbrush now, does it?"

In computing, the class were putting the finishing touches on their websites.

"Now," said Mrs Gorman, who was writing a list on the whiteboard, "make sure you've included all of these features. At the end of the lesson, we'll display everyone's website on the screen and evaluate how successful they are."

Jaden wasn't working on his website. He was on the *Raider's Peril* homepage, looking up player profiles. Katka watched over his shoulder.

"If you type in 'Zircon'," he said, "this is what happens."

Sorry, our net pixies couldn't find a player with that name.

"But how do you know he was banned?" asked Katka, staring at the blank page. It wasn't enough to know that he was gone. She wanted to know what he was up to now.

"Because I reported him," said Jaden as he typed something else. "The admins said I was very brave to turn him in. And guess what else."

The URL he had typed into the address bar was *www.raidertrad.ez*, the website that Zircon had used to sell *Raider's Peril* weapons for Bitcoin.

This site can't be reached.

"It doesn't exist any more," said Jaden.

"He's taken it down?" asked Katka.

"Overnight. Probably knew he was in deep trouble. Don't worry, though. I sent screenshots to the *Raider's Peril* admins. That's why they banned him."

"Right, year six," said Mrs Gorman, interrupting their conversation. "Time to see some of these websites. Jaden and Vijay, since I assume that your website is finished, let's look at that first."

The pair hopped off their chairs. Jaden loaded the website on the whiteboard. If Mrs Gorman had been hoping to catch him out, she was sorely disappointed.

"Woah!" gasped the class, as Jaden and Vijay's masterful creation appeared on the screen.

"It's the latest in website design," Vijay explained, as Jaden clicked various links. "Fully responsive, this website adapts to tablet and phone screens for optimum display." Mrs Gorman nodded, impressed, and drew a big tick on her marking sheet.

Three days passed. Katka played football, and lots of it. Whenever *Raider's Peril* crossed her mind, she remembered that she had no guild left and no Zircon to beat. However, Saturday dawned wet and cold. There was nothing to do.

"Why don't you play that game that you like?" asked Mum as Katka sat on the sofa watching *Rainbow Charm Twins* with Milana.

"Maybe," said Katka.

"I thought you were a guild leader."

"I was."

"I thought you liked raiding."

"I did."

"I thought you had real friends and you didn't want to let them down."

Perian! Katka had forgotten her. They hadn't spoken since Zircon had disappeared. Katka rushed upstairs and quickly logged on. Catanna fizzled into being outside a stronghold which Katka didn't recognise.

"You're back," said a delighted voice. Perian stood there in her blue Brittlestar cape.

"I'm back," Katka agreed.

"I missed you."

"Sorry," said Katka. "It was just, after all that Zircon business..."

"I get it," said Perian. "There was a lot going on."

"So," said Katka. She stared at the stronghold in front of her.

"Do you like it?" asked Perian. "I've been working on improvements non-stop. The new guild members have helped."

"New guild members?" said Katka, as it slowly dawned on her where she was. This was the

Brittlestar stronghold, but better – so much better – than she had left it.

"The Gutvines. Ex-Gutvines. They had nowhere to go after Zircon vanished. I invited them to join the Brittlestars. You don't mind, do you?"

"Don't mind? That's incredible."

"Come and see inside," said Perian. "We have stained glass windows and I've built stables. One of the Gutvines is an expert emu-tamer."

Katka grinned from ear to ear as Catanna followed Perian inside.

Life continued much as usual for the next week. True, Jaden was Star of the Week at school for the first time ever, for his excellent website-building skills, and Katka had a new set of guild members to train but, otherwise, things were much as they ever had been.

Then, one unremarkable morning, the headteacher, Ms Ford, stopped Katka on her way into assembly.

"The photographer is here from the newspaper. Do you want to join Jaden in reception, so that the two of you can have your photo taken?"

"From the newspaper?" said Katka, bewildered.

"Yes. Off you run," said Ms Ford. She gently pushed Katka in the direction of the school office.

Katka walked past lines of pupils queuing outside the hall for assembly. She wondered if she was dreaming. When she reached the office, Jaden was sitting on the squashy, blue chairs and two strange adults stood chatting nearby.

"Ah, Katrina?" said the man with the notebook as Katka approached. Katka nodded. "Fantastic – the woman of the hour. We hear you and your buddy Jaden exposed a cybercriminal from your bedrooms and brought him to justice."

"Uh..." said Katka. She supposed that was one way of putting it.

"Aren't young people today so clever?" said the

reporter. "Hacking codes and modding kilobytes and whatnot."

Katka looked at Jaden, who pulled an exasperated face.

"Tell us – what was it like, uncovering this criminal mastermind, alias Zircon?"

"Well," said Jaden, "I actually mined the webbersphere, but it was Katka who reblogged the hypertext."

The reporter looked like his eyes might pop out.

Katka almost giggled. "Don't listen to Jaden," she said. "I only giffed the terabytes."

"Right," said the reporter. "Yes. Of course. Now, just stand against that wall and my colleague will take your photograph."

Katka folded her hands and tried not to blink as the camera flashed blinding, white light in her face. When the photos were done, the reporter shook their hands.

"Lovely meeting two young computer geniuses such as yourself," he said. "And good luck with those nasty terabytes," he added, with a conspiratorial wink.

As Katka and Jaden pushed open the double doors into the corridor beyond, they burst out laughing.

"The terabytes?" gasped Katka. "What does that mean?"

"Hey, don't ask me, you're the one who giffed them," Jaden cackled.

"We'd better not go into assembly," gasped Katka, "yet."

"You're –" Jaden panted for breath. "– right. There might be –" He looked like he might not get to the end of the sentence.

"Terabytes!"

The pair collapsed against the corridor wall, howling.

The article appeared two days later. At school, Katka felt like a celebrity. Everyone was talking about the news.

"So, this guy was selling weapons for a game?"

"For hundreds of pounds, apparently."

Katka was sitting in her seat, cutting a neat rectangle from the newspaper while talk buzzed all around her.

"You know what this dude did with the money?"

"No, what?"

"He spent it all. Two flashy cars and a smart watch."

"They raided his house. Full of state-of-the-art kit."

"He had six screens. Even his keyboard cost hundreds of pounds."

Zircon had been arrested. It turned out that he was a university student called Graham Turner who had started selling game items to make some spare cash but then, it had got out of hand.

"What would you spend all that money on?" Vijay asked Rick, whose eyes lit up at the idea.

Jaden's shadow loomed over Katka's desk. She put her scissors down. "Ms Ford wants us to say something in assembly," he said. He banged his model diamond axe on the tabletop and some of the glitter flaked off. "Will you do it?"

"I thought you liked making a fool of yourself in front of everyone."

"Yeah." *Bang.* "But only if it's my choice." *Bang.* "Please, Katka?"

"Fine," said Katka, as if it was a great favour.

She didn't mind, really. She was a leader, and leaders spoke out at moments like this.

As a hush fell over the assembly hall, Ms Ford asked, "Katka, as an online crime-fighting mastermind, do you have any words of wisdom?"

"I do, Ms Ford." Katka cleared her throat and spoke in her loudest voice. "There are dangerous people online," she said. "People who hide who they really are, who cheat and lie, and use people to get what they want. When you're online, you have to be careful, just like in real life."

Ms Ford nodded. This was exactly what she had expected Katka to say.

Katka continued. "But there are also good people online. I couldn't have found out the truth without my friends, Jaden and Perian. If we hadn't worked together, we would never have got to the bottom of what Zircon – Graham Turner – was really doing."

Katka put her hand in her pocket. She tightened

her fingers around a crisp newspaper cutting, safely tucked inside. "So what I mean to say is, there are good people and bad people online, just like there are in the real world. That's what I've learned, Ms Ford." The school applauded as Katka and Jaden took their seats.

Katka pulled the cutting from her pocket. It was a picture of a girl in a blazer and tie. She had beautiful, glossy hair and a wide, smiling face. Beneath the picture were printed the words *Parminder Kaur, aged 13.*

Finally, Katka knew Perian's real name.

Above: Parminder Kaur, aged 13.

Catanna Brittlestar

 +1

 +5

 +5

 +3

 +4

 +3

 +3

 +2

How much can you remember about the story? Take this quiz to find out!

1 What is Jaden's avatar called?

a. Zircon

b. Gannymead

c. Xandon

2 What is the name of the online currency used to buy game items illegally?

3 What is Katka's dream weapon?

a. crystal sword

b. fire opal spear

c. topaz spear

Answers: 1. (c) 2. **Bitcoin** 3. (b)

Challenge

Can you unscramble these avatar names to find out who is online?

	ocrdtroorcotc
	anancat
	eaprni
	amgednyna
	snskpocik
	daonxn
	riczno

Answers: Croctordoctor; Catanna; Perian; Gannymead ; Pinksocks; Xandon; Zircon

LOOK OUT FOR THE NEXT BOOK CLUB DELIVERY

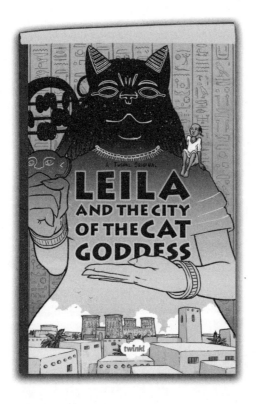

Leila is tired of the hustle and bustle of life in the ancient Egyptian city of cats until, one day, she comes across a very unusual cat with a very unusual problem. Now, it's a race against time to recover a lost magical item from the depths of the pharaoh's tomb. Can Leila and her new companion save the city of the cat goddess before it's too late?

COMING MAY 2021

Can't wait? Get the digital version at twinkl.com/originals

COMING MAY 2021